凸面镜中的自画像
阿什贝利诗集

Self-Portrait in a Convex Mirror
Poems of John Ashbery

[美]约翰·阿什贝利 著

少况 译

雅众文化 出品

目 录

凸面镜中的自画像

1 作为喝醉被抬进邮船的一位

4 每况愈下的局势

6 四十年代电影

7 当你从圣地归来

10 清谈的男人

12 舍赫拉查德

16 彻底的清除

19 大加洛普舞

30 分三部分的诗

34 蓝色中的旅行

38 农场

39 农场（2）

41 农场（3）

42 侏儒

45 世界的影像

47 预感

48 斯图亚特·梅里尔之墓

52 油布

53 河流

54 复杂的感情

56 唯一能拯救美国的东西

59 第十交响乐曲

62 在秋湖上

64 对死亡的恐惧

66 比尔颂

68 立陶宛舞乐队

71 沙桶

72 无从知晓

76 套房

78 童话图画

80 城市下午

81 罗宾汉的谷仓

84 全部和一些

87 仁慈之油

90 凸面镜中的自画像

Self-Portait in a Convex Mirror

117 As One Put Drunk into the Packet–Boat

120 Worsening Situation

122 Forties Flick

124 As You Came from the Holy Land

127 A Man of Words

129 Scheherazade

133 Absolute Clearance

136 Grand Galop

147 Poem in Three Parts

151 Voyage in the Blue

155 Farm

156 Farm II

158 Farm III

159 Hop o' My Thumb

162 De Imagine Mundi

164	Foreboding
165	The Tomb of Stuart Merrill
169	Tarpaulin
170	River
171	Mixed Feelings
173	The One Thing That Can Save America
176	Tenth Symphony
179	On Autumn Lake
181	Fear of Death
183	Ode to Bill
185	Lithuanian Dance Band
188	Sand Pail
189	No Way of Knowing
193	Suite
195	Märchenbilder
197	City Afternoon
198	Robin Hood's Barn
201	All and Some
204	Oleum Misericordiae
207	Self-Portrait in a Convex Mirror

作为喝醉被抬进邮船的一位

我试过每一样东西,只有一些是不朽的,自由的。
在别处,我们坐在一个地方,那里阳光
过滤下来,一次一小点,
等待某个人到来。刺耳的话说出,
随着阳光染黄那棵枫树的绿叶……

所以这就是一切,但隐约地
我感到书页间新的呼吸的颤动,
整个冬天它们闻上去像本旧目录。
新的句子在启动。但夏天
一直不错,尚未过中点,
但饱满,幽暗,带着那个饱满的承诺,
那个时候,一个人不可能再溜达着走开,
即使最心不在焉的也安静下来
观看那件准备好发生的事情。

看一眼玻璃让你驻步,
然后惊恐地继续向前:我是那被察觉的吗?
这一次他们是否注意到我,就是现在的样子,

或者又被推迟了？孩子们

还在玩他们的游戏，云在下午的空中

迅速不耐烦地升起，然后消散，

随着清澈的浓厚的暮色到来。

只有在那里喇叭的

嘟嘟声中，有一片刻，我想到

正式的了不起的事务在开始，精心编排过，

它的色彩凝缩在一瞥中，一支民谣

收留了整个世界，现在，但轻轻地，

依旧轻轻地，但不容置疑，机智老练。

到处都是那些灰色的薄片？

它们是太阳的微粒。你在阳光下已经睡得

比狮身人面像还久，并没有变得更聪明。

进来吧。我以为是一个影子从门上掉下

但只是她又一次来问

我是否进去，并说不要急，万一我不进去。

闪亮的夜接手。熙笃会修士般苍白的月亮

已经爬到了天心，安顿下来，

最终卷入了黑暗的营生。

然后世界上所有小东西全发出了一声叹息，

书籍、报纸、存放在某个地方白纸盒里的

旧袜带和连衫裤纽扣，所有城市的
较低版本压扁在让一切均衡的夜晚底下。
夏天要求并拿走的太多，
但是夜，这克制的，这缄默的，给予大于索取。

每况愈下的局势

像一场暴雨,他说,梳成辫子的色彩
洗刷我,于事无补。或者像一个宴会上
不吃东西的人,因为面对一堆冒烟的
菜肴,他无从选择。切开的手
代表生命,不管它漂泊
到东方还是西方,北方还是南方,永远是
一个陌生人走在我身边。啊,季节,
摊位,炎热,某个乡村节日的郊外
戴深色帽子的江湖骗子们,
他随意提及却从来不说的名字是我的,我的!
有一天,我会对你声称因为你
我如何精疲力尽,但同时,兜风
继续。每一位都可以跟着兜风,
好像是。另外,还有什么?
年度运动会?真的,有些情况下
要穿白色制服,说一种向别人
保密的特殊语言。酸橙
被适当地切成片。我都知道,
但好像无法让它不影响自己,

每天,整天。我试过各种消遣,
读书到深夜,坐火车兜风,
谈恋爱。
   一天,一个男人在我出门时打电话,
还留了言:"你搞得满拧,
从头到尾。幸运的是,还有时间
来改变局势,但你必须出手要快。
方便时尽早来见我。但请不要
告诉谁。你生命外很多事情要靠它。"
当时我对它置若罔闻。近来,
我一直盯着老派的格子呢,摸着
上了浆的白领子,想着是否有办法
把它们真的再次变白。我妻子
认为我在奥斯陆——法国奥斯陆,没错。

四十年代电影

粉刷过的墙上百叶窗的影子,
虎皮兰和仙人掌的影子,石膏动物像,
将镜头明晃晃的凝视中的悲情聚焦
成惘然,一个洞,像太空中的黑洞。
她戴着胸罩,穿着内裤,侧身到窗前:
拉开!窗帘向上。易碎的街景映入眼帘,
薄片一样的行人知道自己要去哪里。
窗帘慢慢落下,百叶板慢慢向上倾斜。

为什么它一定总要这样结束?
一个露天平台,女人在读书,她头发蓬乱,
关于她没说的一切将我们拉回她身边,和她一起
进入仅仅靠那个夜晚无法解释的寂静。
图书馆的寂静,带通讯簿的电话的寂静,
但我们也没必要重新发明这些:
它们已消失在一个故事的情节里,
"艺术"部分——知道什么重要细节要省略,
如何塑造人物。事物太真实,
无法备受关注,因此是虚假的,现在却占据整个页面,
室内和户外一起成为你的一部分,
当你发现自己从未停止过嘲笑死亡,
那背景,门廊边缘上暗黑的葡萄藤。

当你从圣地来

自纽约州西部
坟墓在它们的衬套里可安好
八月下旬的空气里是否有一丝惊慌
因为老头又尿裤子了
在那里转过身去躲开下午晚些时候的怒视
仿佛这个也能掩耳盗铃
这个现在的任何东西是不是
而这个怎么可以是
你现在所谓的神奇的解决方案
无论什么迷住了你一动不动
像这个如此漫长穿过黑暗的季节
直到现在女人们穿一身海军蓝出来
虫子们从堆肥中出来去死
这是任何季节的结束

你如此精确地阅读那里
坐着不想被打扰
当你从那圣地来
还有其它什么地球附属地的标志在你身上

什么固定标志在十字路口

什么样的冷漠在大街上

那里一切都在低语

什么样的语调在树篱丛中

什么样的口气在苹果树下

编号的土地向远处延伸

你的房子建在明天里面

但肯定不是在审查过什么是

正确的之前也不会降临

在人口普查

和写下姓名之前

记住你可以随时离开

如同离开其它时代其它正在发生的场景

某个来得太迟的人的历史

时机现在成熟了而格言

正在孵化随着季节变化颤动

最终仿佛那个让人产生可怕的兴趣的东西

正在天空中发生

但太阳在落下阻止你看到它

从夜里象征涌现

它的叶片像鸟同时落在一棵树下

再一次被拿起摇晃

在虚弱的愤怒中放下
知道就像脑子知道它永远不会发生
不在这里不在过去的昨天
只是在填满自己的今天的缝隙中
当空虚被分发
在现在是什么时候的想法里
当那个时间已经过去

清谈的男人

他的箱子引起了兴趣,
但很少同情;它比最初的
样子要小。最初的荨麻
是否和发展成讽刺短文的东西
有任何区别?三面围拢,
第四面敞开,朝向天气的洗刷,
出口和入口,戏剧化的动作,表示
要像弯折的杂草那样加上标点符号,
当花园积满了雪?
啊,这本来应该是另一个,相当别样的
娱乐,而不是我把脸转过去时
嘴巴里的金属味道,密度黑如火药,
以草书继续的角度,
在意想不到的地方是玫瑰红,如同手指
摁住一本啪地合上的书。

真相那些纷乱纠缠的版本
细心梳理好,疙瘩撕开,
铺展开来。在面具后面,

仍然是一种陆地上的欣赏,关于什么
是精美的,很少出现的,一旦出现,
已然在微风上死去,而风把它带到
语言的门槛。故事在讲述中耗尽。
所有的日记都是一样的,清楚,冷漠,
并带着持续冷漠的前景。它们横着
放置,与大地平行,
如同不造成负担的死者。是时候重读一遍这个,
过去从你的指缝间溜走,但愿你在这里。

舍赫拉查德

没有得到理性之谜的支撑,
水汇集在正方形的石头集水池里。
陆地干燥。下面流动着
水。鱼活在井里。叶子,
一种忧虑的绿,潦草地被写在光线上面。坏的
小旋花和难闻的豚草不知为何忘记在这里繁盛。
一个取之不尽的衣柜已经放好,任凭每一次
新的事件使用。它现在可以成为自己。
白天几乎不情愿衰败
而缓慢下来伸展出新的大街
它们并不侵犯空间,但和我们一起生活在这里。
其他的梦来了,又离去,当彩色的动词
和形容词的河岸退缩,躲避光线
在阴凉处对自己匮乏一种方法进行调理,
但最重要的是,她爱那些语助词,
它们把同一种类的物体转换成
一个个特定的,每一个不同,
在自己门类的里面,又脱离出去。
在所有这些涌现中,没有潮水的

迹象，只有空气令人愉悦的颤动，
所以事物好像都出现在里面，无论是
刚过去的还是马上到来的。一切在邀请。
花朵沿着夜巷如此这般呈现
轮廓，当很少看得见，而
它们的故事听上去声音响过
虫鸣和殿后的棍子噪声，
一直滚着它进入一个白天的新事实。
这些是用来被视为随意在
言归正传之前的寒暄，
但它们坚持己见，而它们
如此固执地想和其它的保持一致
（如同白鸟长时间闪光，拒绝
与白天同归于尽）以致没人知道这表现
主要乐章的弯曲是作为一个坚定的
偏离，一片慢慢成为一座山脉的平原。

所以每一位都发现自己困在网里
是一种时尚，所有想挣脱的努力
让他卷得更深，无情地，既然所有
存在在那里要讲述的，极速射过，
从边境到边境。这里是被看成
斑驳阳光的石头，那里是故事，

关于祖父母,关于活力四射的年轻冠军
(台词曾经给了另一位,现在
又给回到新的发言人),晚餐和集会,
旧居里的光线,房间彼此
插入的隐秘方式,但一切
都是时间自我审视的警觉,
因为复杂的故事里没有什么生长在外面:
讲诉时刻的伟大性依旧不明朗,
直到它丰富的事件,痛苦混合着快乐,
在突然绽放那准确的一刻
黯淡,它的成长,一首静止的挽歌。

一些故事比建造者的王朝寿命还长
但它们的回声是被锁定的自己,成为
终究只是记忆的期待,
因为可能性受到限制。最后
看到的是良善之人得到福报,
而不公正的注定永远绕着自己的
错误被灼伤,反正愈加悲伤和智慧。
在这些极端之间,其他人像我们一样
在蒙混过关,不确定,但天真地承担着
他们的作用,作为必须被牢记的
小人物。正是我们制造了这片

丛林,并称之为空间,命名每一条根,
每一条蛇,为了那个名字的声音,
随着它沉闷地叮当撞击我们的快乐,
漠不关心就是那快乐。而它们会是什么,
如果没有观众限制无数的
通行证和刷卡,恢复到不错的幽默,当它散布进
不透风的傍晚空气中?所以在某种方式上,
虽然算数是错的
平衡得以恢复,因为它
保持平衡,知道它胜出,
而那个同样错误犯两次的人被免除了责任。

彻底的清除

> 这就是,先生们,上帝给宇宙的景象……
> ——波舒哀

他看见墙上的画,
只是真相的一个样本。
但一个人永不餍足,
真相并不令人满意。

在某个模糊的酒店房间里,
线状的斑点,当黄昏
抬起它们,是白天和黑夜。

而远在海洋上方
那个愿望坚持做一个在家的梦
云朵或鸟儿睡在
不着边际的波浪的水槽里。

那些时代,当一匹驽马沿着
运河岸似乎是无关的,而真相:

在时间与其它时间有关的
最好样本中最好的。

再一次忍受光线被替换
冒着烟下沉
"他冲天的勇气如此大，
他的智慧如此浩瀚，
他的命运如此辉煌。

如同一个人看见的鹰，
无论是在半空中翱翔，
还是落在某块岩石上，
总是目光犀利地环顾四周，
如此必然地落在猎物上面，
一个人能躲过它的爪子，
只要能躲过它的眼睛。"

它会如何更加清晰，
仅仅游手好闲，很少想象
（阳光下一只猫的皮毛）：
让一栏数字
移动，加减自己
（细枝，数字，字母）

如此等等到达中位深度……

直到某个小镇的房间
里面一次会议的结果
握紧,松开,
朝着总有一天玩具
被最后收起的慌乱表情。

"我收起幼稚的东西。
正是为了这个我来到里弗赛德
在这里生活了三年,
现在终于到达一种并非不确定的
结局,或一些人愿意称之为成熟。"

用它终极的保证
逗弄拂动的光线
它弯曲的微笑严肃
"像那头鹰
盘旋,盘旋,然后落下。"

大加洛普舞

所有事物似乎都是对自身的提及
根源于它们的名字扩展到其它的指涉物。
浩大地,春天又一次开始。锦带花在火锤打的空气里
做它尘土飞扬的事情。垃圾桶靠着栏杆
堆在一起,随着郁金香打哈欠,裂开,凋落。
而今天是星期一。今天的午餐是:西班牙煎蛋卷,
　生菜西红柿沙拉,
果冻酱,牛奶和饼干。明天的:牛肉碎圆面包,
奶油玉米饼,炖西红柿,米布丁和牛奶。
我们偷来的名字并没移除我们:
我们已经在它们前面移动了一点,
而现在又到了等待的时刻。
只是等待,那等待:什么打发它们之间的时间?
它是另一种等待,等待那等待结束。
没有什么占去了它应有的时间,
那等待被深植于刚刚发挥作用的事物之中。
没有什么是部分不完整的,但那等待
像气候一样投入了一切。
现在几点了?

有什么事重要吗?

有的,因为你必须等待着看它到底什么样子,

这个事件绕过拐角

不会像任何别的东西,真的

不足为奇:它太充裕了。

水

从空调滴落

在下面经过的那些人身上。它是我们小镇的一景。

哕。呕吐。哕哕哕。更多呕吐。牵着狗散步的

一个人远远地在说着所有这些如何

把分钟变成一小时,小时变成

一天的时间,一天天变成一月月,那些容易把握的
 实体,

而一月月变成四季,它对我们的时间概念而言,

是相当不一样的,陌生的。最好是一月月——

它们几乎是一个个人——而不是这些抽象概念,

像云石粉一样筛过工作室里未完成的作品,

让每一样东西都衰老,性格化。

最好清扫委员会开始关心

某一项,现在略大于某种过时风格的

一个特征——檐口和拱肩

出自那个可能缺乏真正特征的

记忆模糊的整体。但如果一个人可以捡起它，
带到那边去，放下，
然后这件作品最后被赎回，
在微笑的广阔天空下，
它不偏爱什么，但以相同的方式
只对那些寻找过它的人是荣誉。

狗吠叫，商队继续路过。
那些词语的上面有一种红润，
但它们没重量，承载正在说着的过去。
"大好时光，"你想道，"可以出门：
刚入夜凉爽，但不是
太什么。人们，带着宠物招摇穿过
草坪和空地，仿佛这些不知为何也是不可估量的，
在回家过一个关在门后的
体面的私人生活之前，它不关任何人的事。
它对其他人是有点重要的
但只是因为它让他们意识到他们的尊重把自己
带到多远。没人敢闯入。
这是一个夜晚，和其它许多的一样，
天空现在有点不耐心等今天结束，
像无聊的女售货员从一只脚换到一只穿长袜不穿
  鞋的脚。"

这些卡其色短裤挂在外面的绳子上，
风在它们中间翻腾，我们永远不会去发表声明吗？"
我们总是路过的某些楼房从未被提及——
事情正在失控。
只要一个人有点明白每一样东西都守本分
安然无事，但随着每一个新的
到达和出发，在半黑暗中如此强烈地重叠，
是有点疯狂。太糟糕了，我的意思是，了解每一个
   只有飞逝的一秒钟，
必须被对无特征整体不完全的了解取代，
如同某本袖珍世界历史，如此笼统，
以致于去构成一声啜泣或哀号，不涉及
对定义的任何尝试。而小时代
担负了一种与故事不成比例的重要性，
因为它不可能再松开，但必须留在手上，
无限期地，像一个无人曾经使用的急救箱，
或字典里永远不会有人查找的一个字。
蛋白沙司在凝固；与此同时
我不仅有自己的历史要担心，
还要被迫烦恼，为与未完成的大概念相关的
不充分的细节，这些概念，永远无法将自己带到
   存在的
意义上，无论有没有我的帮助，如果有什么会到来。

正是商队行进离开,

进入一个抽象的夜,没有

明确的目标看得见,确实也不在乎,

才让这次停顿分开,为何要匆忙

朝相反的方向疾驰而去,去往无穷远的另一头?

因为事情会在犹豫不决的时刻意味深长地变硬。

我无法决定走在哪个方向

但我无所谓,我不妨

决定去爬一座山(它看上去几乎是平的)

也可以决定回家,

或去一个酒吧或餐厅,或去某个朋友的

家,他迷人,和我一样没用,

因为这些停顿应该就是生活,

因为它们将钢钉插入孔中,仿佛在说

试图逃跑是没用的,

反正一切都在这里。而它们的侧面陡峭,滑,蔑视

任何连续性的概念。正是这个

将我们带回到似乎是真正的历史里面——

光泽暗淡、杂乱无章的那种,没有日期,

从一棵树空心的树干里对外面说话,

警告那些只是礼貌的人离开,或那些人,他们的命运

没留给他们时间找碴儿争吵手段问题,

那个不是目的，不过却……确切地说它到底是什么，
关于现在几点，天气，它让人们煞费苦心地在日记中
　记录它，
为了让后来的人们读到？
当然，这是因为此刻击中你的
光线或幽暗是希望
以它成熟的、女主人的整个形态出现，考虑了所有
　事情，
然后根据大小重新分配它们，
以便如果一个人无法说这是事情应该已然发生的
自然方式，至少他不可能有抱怨的理由，
等同于已经到达了终点，如此
期待是明智的，并因为满足期待，或不抱期待得到
　改善。
但是我们说，它不会有这样的结局，
只要我们被遗弃，没地方可去。
然而它已经结束，我们已经成为我们完成的东西。

现在是早晨的冲动让我的
手表嘀嗒作响。如同一个人从一堆
毯子底下探出头，好坏不分，
所以这纠缠一起的不可能的毅然决然和优柔寡断：
渴望开心，闹出声响，如此给厕所

墙上已经几乎无法辨认的灌木丛般的涂鸦添彩。

有人要来抓你：

那个邮递员，或一个男管家进来，托盘上有一封信，

内容是去改变一切，但同时，

一个人要去担心自己的味道或头皮屑或丢失的

  眼镜——

但愿前奏会结束，但它没完没了。

但是存在着这样的慰藉：

如果最后是不值得去做，我还没做；

如果景象惊到了我，我还没看见什么；

如果胜利代价高昂，我还没赢过。

所以从这一天，到处是关于

正在山的另一面完成的事情的流言中

留下了一个核，一种依旧完美的可能性

可以被无限期地保留。然而

产前阵痛的呻吟震耳欲聋；一个人必须

起身，出门，与它相安无事。早晨是给像你这样的

  娘娘腔的，

但真正的磨难,那些把男孩和男人分开的,晚些到来。

俄勒冈对我们更友善。街道

提供了各种各样的方向，给脚，

给出售色情书刊的书店。但是后来

一个人嗅到空气中一丝淡淡的疯狂味道。
他们全上了车，开走了，
像一部电影里的结尾。所以它最终没有区别，
无论这是结尾，还是它在别处：
假如它必须在某个地方，它也可以
在这里，在一个之上。这里，一如别处，
四月提出了新的建议，一个人不妨
随着它们一起向前，尤其是考虑到
午夜蓝光，把自己由里翻到外，
为注意力提供了某种奇异之物，一件东西
不是它自己，虫蚋在我眼前旋转，
速度难以置信，没有活力。毕竟太显著了，
不会那么毫无意义。然后继续前往沙漠里的
下午，自己被清理干净，地点
几乎是全新的，因为剥去了口香糖纸等等。
但我在试图告诉你一件发生在我身上的
奇怪的事情，但这样讲诉它是不可能的，
靠着让它真正地发生。它以碎片的形式飘走了，
剩下一个人坐在院子里，
试图写诗，
用怀亚特和塞莱留下来的，
拿起来又放下，
如同这么多绚丽多彩的原材料，

仿佛它多少总是会发生,

而与此同时,既然我们在向前进,

它肯定会不顾一切发生

在星期天,当时,剩下你一个人坐在

阴凉处,那里和往常一样有点太凉。

所以,有一种旋转扑向你,从不太深的

空无处,那个"鸡巴"字眼,或一些其它,兄弟
   姐妹类的词语,

从它们那里没有太多可期待的,虽然这些

就是等了你如此久,最后离开的那些,已经放弃了
   希望。

在一个人的嗓音里有一种绝望的语调,恳求它们,

与此同时,强度变薄,把它的观点

变得尖锐,那就是它要问的东西。

整个晚上,一个人一直在等它,

在睡眠最后关闭了所有作为观众

而来的那些人的眼睛和耳朵之前。

不过,那诗歌有时确实会发生,

但愿是在书信的折痕中,

它们包好,装在阁楼的箱子里——你忘记了自己
   曾经拥有的东西,

那又有什么关系呢,

那个报酬,如此精确的剂量,

以至于看上去像一个有悖常理的判断落了实。
你忘了怎么会有一阵新鲜空气
藏在那片混乱中。当然,你的遗忘
是一个迹象,正好表明它对你有多重要:
"它一定是重要的。"
谎言落下,像亚麻线从空中
落在美国各处,而它们一些当然是真实的这一事实
并非如此不重要,以至于可以用来证明翻腾的
正确的愉悦下面那整个疯狂的组织力量是合理的。
塞莱,你的诗琴正遭遇神经麻痹的发作,
但,又有了值得吟咏的事物,
而这是其中一样,只是我不会梦想着侵扰
那疯狂的完整性,抢劫起源于其中
依旧潮湿的花园里那万能的仁爱:
在咬牙切齿的空隙之间,你恶毒的小回旋诗。
去问一头猪正发生什么。去吧。问他。
道路就像在消失,
并且在远处也没那么远。地平线一定是被抬高了。
所以正是靠瘸着腿小心翼翼
从一天到另一天,一个人走近了一座破旧的
 石头圆塔,
它蜷伏在一条沟壑的凹陷处,
没有门窗,却有许多旧车牌,

钉在一条裂缝上方，缝太细，手腕都伸不进去，
还有一个招牌："金宝牌猪肉豆。"
从那时起进入：焦虑色彩的天空，情感退缩，
随着整个事情甚至开始惊吓到你，
它的发起者和推动者。地平线返回，
这次是作为一个认可的微笑，礼貌，毫无疑问。
学校毕业似乎是多久以前的事
不过它不可能这么久：
一个人走了这么短的距离。
样式变化不大，
我还有一件毛衣，一两样别的那时的东西。
好像就是昨天，我们看了
里面有几头牛的电影
然后向你旁边的一位转过身去，他打着嗝
当早晨看见一种石榴石豆青的秩序举荐
自己，自无尽的陈腐，像科幻小说里的叙事疙瘩。
不可能不被那些人戴着的那个
小数字打动，它暗示着他们应该被提升到这个或
　　那个权力。
但现在我们在恐怖角，陆路小径
不可逾越，浓雾悬浮在大海之上。

分三部分的诗

1. 爱

"我曾经让一个家伙口我。
我有点从那次经历中退缩。
现在,几年过去,我不带情感
想起它。没有再来一次的渴望,
也没宿醉的感觉。也许如果情况合适,
它可能还会发生,但我不知道,
我只是有其它要思考的事情,
更重要的事情。谁和什么上床
并不重要。感情是重要的。
我通常思考感情,它们填满我的生活,
像风,像翻滚的云,
在满是云的天空,层层叠叠的云。"

无名的灌木横穿一片田野,
它去年没有排干水,
今年也没有,像波浪
在湖的尽头落空,

每一个都轻轻叹息,
你是否肯定这就是纯净的日子
亮着立灯的意图所在?
有这么多不同的工作:
选一个,或一个的零头,就足够了。
日子,带着自己的目的,在别处会是蓝色的。
一个人必须记住一件事。
没必要知道那个东西是什么。
所有东西都是明显的,无人知晓。
这一天受煎熬,带着良知,
影子,涟漪,灌木丛,旧车。

良心对你而言就如同众所周知。
不可知的变得广为人知。
熟悉的东西似乎在远处。

2. 勇气

穿菱形窗格子衬衫,
就这样出发:
一个胡扯的早晨
离家不太远(家

是简陋的一居室公寓,

由城市拥有并经营),

旅程的平均碎片

比最初以为的少,

开放水域的味道,

水槽,特殊的坑。

一切再一次及时

转回去,为了傍晚的扭矩:

我们本来可以做的是如此多,

我们确实做了如此多。

杂草如摩天大楼,衬着天空蓝色的拱顶:

它在哪里终结?这是什么?这些人是谁?

我是自己吗?还是一株说话的树?

3. 我爱大海

没有承诺,但有很多

亲密在泛黄的土地缩小的方式中。

这部分因为某种缘故不是

很受欢迎:房屋需要修葺,

院子里的小汽车太新。

封闭的斜坡做梦且健忘,

在没有特征的树木中

有几小片欢快而温暖。

我的梦变得迟钝。

今天早上醒来,我先注意到

你不在那里,然后催促

自己慢慢返回梦中:

这些火车,人群,海滩,驰骋

在幸福中,因为它们的多彩多姿

已过时,但还在那里,在外面某个地方,

在侧院里,也许。

常春藤正在覆盖一整面墙。

时间更加黑暗,

在现在与它有关的方面,因为快速的原因进入一切。

我们又可以睡在一起,但那个无法

带回大海这些险梦的好处,

那一切碰撞,那失明,那与大海

附近其它日子联系在一起的血,

虽然它流个不停,像正午的失明。

蓝色中的旅行

如同在一个早春的节日里
潮滩在演习,空中很快在模仿:
船只,帽子出现。而那些,
读别人心思的人们,就在眼前。但是
要了解他们我们必须躲开他们。

所以,生命渗进我们的黑暗,
信守它那部分承诺。但是假如
房屋,此刻耸立着,破败,荒凉,又如何:
这难道不是也美丽绝伦吗?
因为海市蜃楼曾经是的,生命一定是。

盛会,变得愈发好奇,抵达
一个最终的转折点。现在一切都不会
是暗的,而是相反,充满了如此多的光
它看上去是暗的,因为事物现在被密密麻麻包在一起。
我们是用牙齿看见它的。而一旦这个

遥远的角落转过去,一切

再不会成为新的,随着理想的事物来到我们这里,
它们将以旧的方式栖居在我们里面,
然而,在拥有中,我们将成长,超越它,
进入一个上了深蓝瓷釉的天空和刚毛金色星星的
　混合体。

日期进来的方式
没有意义,它从未有过。
它应该已经警告过你
要更加仔细地去听风下面的
话语,当风朝我们吹来。

也许,沉入那只激情四射的眼睛珍珠似的污渍,
那些时刻开始看上去像是它们所遭遇的排泄物,
一个颜色不再重要的时代。
它们对我们来说是作为我们注定不会获得的品质,
因为太远离我们封闭的状态。

理想的话,它的鸣响
会具有一件回想起来的事情的魅力,
没有化身,或者更遥远,像某个闻所未闻的
国度里的一次灾难,我们的关切
也只是一长串重要事实中的另一个事实。

你和我和那条狗
在这里,这才是现在重要的。
其它时间,事情会发生,没有可能涉及现在的我们,
而这是好事,一件真实的东西,垂直于地面,
如同最新鲜、最不复杂和最早的记忆。

我们拥有他们全部,那些人们,而现在他们拥有我们。
他们的决定受到限制,等待我们主动出击。
但现在我们已经这么做了,结果高深莫测,仿佛
一个单一的含义从茎干上动摇了整个宇宙。
我们时髦地受这个新的边缘困扰,它在过去似乎是

有限的,而现在似乎是无限的,虽然被包围在对
　任何影响
我们的事情的逐渐怀疑中。也许过时的时髦少一些
　贫瘠,
某样更被期待的东西,相比这个
无云的天空下果园中的早晨,
这种痛苦的新鲜,每一样东西完全是它自己。

也许所缺少的就是时间。
人们掩护我们,他们年长,

曾经沧桑。他们不想和我们搅在一起,
只想死去,彻底了结。
不和所有正在伴随他们的一切合拍,

但和它们一起深入事物的内部活着。
毕竟,重要的是文明,他们似乎
在说,我们和别人一样是它的一部分,
只是我们更少,甚至根本不思考它,直到某个
傻瓜在黄昏时冲着森林里面大声报告

关于我们知道但不在乎的某样东西的消息,
随着远方的城堡在为欢快的马蹄声
兴高采烈,将秃鼻乌鸦直接放飞进完美无暇的空中,
与此同时,把它的影子越来越重地投在
镜子般的河面上,围住里面有三个人影的小船。

农场

一场旷日持久的等待也是夜晚。
奇怪,白色的围栏桩竟然
延绵不断,一种轻声的责备
随白天结束消沉
虽然几何学不变,
一件裸体一样的东西,在漫长
一段的结尾。"迥然不同。"
好啊。那"根本不一样的东西"亦是如此,
从望远镜错的一端看过去,
抢劫那个酒吧。

和女孩一起生活
被踢进一堆破事。
有一种待办事宜的六月末,
来来往往,
在事情放下之前。
但它留了下来,像她眉头
微皱,或大黄和蜀葵
滴水的叶子,
也是瞬间的失败。
没有人笑到最后。

农场（2）

我当时在想

既然花朵被

    遗忘

一条全新的边界

绕着旧的后退

淹没了它以前的好主意

它们也在错误下耕犁

转着锡的漩涡：超载的

渡轮缓慢地驶离码头

这些可是折角的东西

杂草你怎么称呼它们

这些东西放着像下午

快结束时要读的邮件

邮递员带来的东西

我想报名参加

研究中心的

新课程

一个格子花样的硬壳

洞是一团团黑暗

横放在路上

你无法再那样走出去很远

他们说孩子们在毁坏

林子的内部

    烧焦的橙子

说它壮观

但是它没有

将我们带出去进入公海

只是带到一条河的中央

摸索着去向何方。

农场（3）

小波浪击打

黑石头。妻子读着

来信。没有什么不可逆转：

指向入侵的腰豆炖牛肉

最后的咝咝声。

很快，油已经

取代了你周围

黑暗的位置。一切如

所说，但无论如何结果总是不对劲：

这里一小部分，无关紧要的地方口齿不清。

它必须通过一个

最后的缺口呈现：梨树和花朵

一面最终的树脂墙

在你的身份温和的气候里

晒太阳。阴郁的富饶

要被照料。

侏儒

大饭店,翩翩起舞的姑娘们,
在"幻灭"的面纱下敦促着
这行为到今天或某个其它日子。
没有一个日子,在乳品公司
发出的日历里
让你疯狂地拥有它像
梦中一个正在做梦的女人的身体:
被抓时,整个在顶上翻了过来,
茎太细长,顶又太松散,笨重,
因为梦的细叶子满脸通红。
一辆辆汽车,金属丝帽子,
蛋糕晚餐,多情的孩子们,
走在孤独的向下的梦之径上,
然后再也看不见了。
什么事情,温蒂妮?
在摧毁一切的暴风雨的喧嚣中,
音符现在几乎听不见,
第三个愿望尚未说出。

我记得在四月一个幽暗的梦里

遇见你,你或某个姑娘,

愿望的项链是活的,绕着你的脖子喘气。

在那片幽暗的无明中,它的

明亮变成沙子,在正午的阳光下上了盐釉,

我们彼此不认识,也不知道哪个部分

属于另一半,在暴雨的电闪雷鸣中被抛掷。

只有渐渐地,意味着我们的身体的那一堆,

穿戴着我们的自我,凹成形显现,

但是断断续续地,仿佛穿过幽暗的迷雾,

被涂抹在雾上。没有更糟糕的时候了,

然而一切都在渴望着,虽然早已被渴望过。

那个时刻,作为自己的纪念碑,

没有人看见和知道,它在那里。

那时间也褪色了,夜晚

柔软成平滑的螺旋形,或夜里的树叶。

附近有睡觉的木屋,黑着的灯笼,

夜间友好的一盘牛奶,留给精灵,

他们否则不会那么友好和善:

白床单的友谊,用牛奶缝补。

而总是有一片开阔的黑暗,一个名字在里面

一遍又一遍喊叫:阿丽亚娜!阿丽亚娜!

是否为了这个你将姐妹们从睡梦中领回，
而现在蓝胡子的他已经战胜了你？
但这也许最好：让
那些姐妹们偷偷溜进宝石蓝的
头发，那上升的白天。
仍然有其他编造的国度
我们能永远躲在那里，
被永恒的渴望和悲伤所耗尽，
吸吮着雪葩，哼着小调，起着名字。

世界的影像

被一个注意到的许多:
被注意到的一个,把自己和许多搞混了,
却又把自己看成一个个体
在两个固定点之间移动。
这样的目光,随着勇气投掷出去
把你钉在你下午的巢穴里,仅仅是一种反射,
一篇讲演,在完全由舞台指示构成的剧本里,
因为那里碰巧有一个给它准备的洞
不幸的是,不到百分之零点五的人
把猜测的手势认作货币
(它确实是,尽管是膨胀的)
而目光落在尖塔顶上,
带着和一只鸟几乎一致的兴趣。

他们已经从波士顿搬迁到这里,
那两个人。(一个,捆扎均匀的
许多中的典型样本,
另一个躲闪,孤僻古怪,
玩味它,当他不能
变得更好或更年轻。)

天气使他们只能干些琐屑之事:
给新闻分类,缝缝补补。
大扑克脸撞击着他们。而且兴高采烈,
能够活生生地责备
他们得到的某种新事物。
蚊子收集信息:"你是否知道
最后时辰的骑墙派?"
他们真实的平声,
一个"休息日"的标志,
公共汽车相当快地在附近的岛屿上行驶,
也注册了,按照他的计划。

走一条你以前从未见过的小路,
以为你知道这个区域
(许多人感觉他们击退了睡眠)。
"一些领班坚持到
队伍的尽头
不过那是在书挡之间。"
音符最终敲响,
用足够的力量,但如同一声霹雳,
可以想象到的最响亮的。
而他们留下来要好好谈谈。

预感

湖面一阵微风——花瓣状的
游乐园效果避免了假如我们在这里
我们会在何处的逗人的轮廓。
我们被炸得心思全无,我认为
这里的路太近了,太充满
涌动的情感。不可能。
彻底毁灭先发生在中心,
现在围绕着边缘。一个丑陋的大家伙
戴着牙箍,把一个伸手去拿盖着神剑
图案的铂金斧头的小家伙踢得屁滚尿流:
真的只是丛林。日间酒吧里
挤满了人,但夜晚在口袋和侧通风口里
有更多的意义。我感到好像
有人刚刚带给我一个方程式。
我说:"我回答不了这个——我知道
它是真的,请相信我,
我能看见证据,崇高,无形,
在远高于条纹雨棚的天空中。我只是明白
我想要它继续,没有
任何人受到伤害,在我和我
这一边的夜晚之间重新洗牌。"

斯图亚特·梅里尔之墓

这是三月的第一个傍晚
他们已经拿走了植物。

玛莎·胡普尔想要一朵大大的"玄秘曲的"绣球
让她的纸牌派对到处散发着
姬琪的味道:地下室无法
支撑所有那些狂野。

花色小蛋糕已经离开。

然后少校起身说道:
新保守主义正在
你们身旁坐下。
一旦公共汽车滑出经过佩雷尔广场
我捕捉到了镜头盖的影像:紫丁香
不会造成多大差别它说了。

否则在巴黎你为何
从来不太赞成我的宠物疗法。

我曾经提到过一种痔疮缓解剂

你不愿尝试也不承认试过其它的。

现在我们过着没有彼此的生活,准确地说是

没有彼此相处。我们每一个人确实

生活在那个难题里面

我们不称之为活着

同时关闭又敞开。

知识会有害吗?

颁布一道命令如何?我想到

让自己听由法庭的怜悯。

他们在把植物带回来

逐一地

在天空、大地和今天的缝隙中。

"我已经被你的风格吸引。你的作品里似乎有一种彻底自由表达和意象恣肆的样子,有点有趣又令人困惑。我读过你的一首诗之后,总是想一而再地读它。我的不成熟似乎阻止我理解你的意思。"

"我真的想知道你做什么来让你的诗歌产生'吸力',而好奇的读者,总是有点困惑,回到你的诗中去获得一种更清晰的洞察力。"

卡农曲式在落下
逐一地
包括帕赫贝尔的名曲
弗兰克钢琴和小提琴奏鸣曲的最后乐章。
一种新的隐士的保守主义
而且出现同样的戒断症候怎么办?

让我们继续吧
但是过去怎么办

因为它完全由片段搭建起来。
每一个傍晚我们走出去看
他们在寺庙进展得如何。
看着一件如何加在
另一件上是有趣的。
至少它不是可怕的,
像在一座医院里面,然后真的发现
在里面是什么样子。
所以一个人不想把这一页包括
在我们生活的片段中
正如它的意义就要凝结
在我们周围的空气里:

"父亲!""儿子!""父亲,我以为我们已经在
　爱琴海
蔚蓝和暗黄的飞机里失去了你:
现在你好像真的回来了。"
"只是暂时回来,儿子,只是暂时回来。"
我们现在可以进到里面去了。

油布

在下午晚些时候空虚之前
让事物平静地
爆发活跃
是一种意志力
将它从一千扇公寓窗户
收到的景象闪烁回去
就在夜晚
它的信号逐渐消失前

河流

它觉得这些概括

配不上自己,却又

靠它们推着向前。对面

被投入阴影,这一面

扎进自尊。然而中心

不断坍塌,重新成形。

一张野餐桌旁,这对夫妇(可是

这个季节野餐为时尚早)

周围摇曳着河流

关于如何避免可能的无聊

并不自知的知识,以及太多

直觉的斑点,整个场景

被玻璃围在后面。"这个季节,"

她说,"为时尚早。"一只鹰飘过。

"送每个人回城里吧。"

复杂的感情

一阵煎香肠的香味

袭击了感官,伴随着一张旧的,几乎看不清的

照片,里面好像是姑娘们在一架

旧战斗轰炸机周围休息,大约 1942 年制造的。

怎么向这些姑娘们解释,如果她们确实是的话,

这些露丝们、琳达们、帕蒂们和希拉们,

关于已经在我们的社会结构中

发生的巨大变化,改变了其中

所有事情的纹理? 然而

不知为何她们看上去仿佛她们知道,除了

看清楚她们是这么难,还很难弄清

她们脸上到底是什么样的表情。

姑娘们,你们有什么爱好? 哼,靠,

她们中一位也许会说,这家伙烦死我了。

我们走吧,去什么地方,

穿过服装中心的峡谷,

去一家小咖啡馆,喝杯咖啡。

我不生气,这些我想像出来的

东西(就这么称呼)似乎如此轻视我,

对我这么熟视无睹。无疑，它无论如何
都是复杂的常规调情中的一部分。但这个关于服装中心的
谈话呢？当然那是加利福尼亚阳光
抽打她们，还有旧的木条箱，她们在上面
披挂自己，它的唐老鸭标志褪色
到辨识度的极限。
也许她们在说谎，但更有可能的是她们
脑子小，无法保留大量信息。
连一件事实也不行，也许。这就是她们
为何认为自己是在纽约。我喜欢她们的
外观、举止和感觉。我好奇
她们怎么做到这样的，但不打算
再浪费什么时间去琢磨她们。
我已经忘记了她们
直到有一天，在不太遥远的未来，
当我们相遇，可能是在一个现代机场的休息厅，
她们看上去就像这张照片拍摄时一样令人惊讶地
 年轻，清新，
但充满矛盾的想法，愚蠢的以及
有价值的，但全部涌入我们思想的表面，
随着我们喋喋不休说着天空和天气和变化的森林。

唯一能拯救美国的东西

有什么东西是核心的吗?
抛在陆地上的果园,
城市森林,乡村种植园,膝盖高的小山?
地名是核心的吗?
榆树林,阿德科克角,故事书农场?
随着它们同时在视线高度涌来,
将自己敲打进眼睛,它们已经有了足够的
谢谢你,不再谢谢你。
它们带着夹杂着黑暗的风景渐次来了
潮湿的平原,发展过快的郊区,
公民自豪感出了名的地方,公民默默无闻的地方。

这些连接到我对美国的描述
但果汁在别处。
今天早晨,当我早饭后走出
你的房间,回望和前望的视线
平行交叉,回望光线,
前望不熟悉的光线,
它是否是我们的行为,是否是

材料，生命的木材，或者生活的，
我们正在衡量，计数？
一种很快被遗忘的情绪
在光线交叉的大梁中，市中心的阴凉里
在这个再次捕获了我们的早晨？

我知道我编织了太多我自己
对事物被折断的感知，随着它们浮现。
它们是私人的，将永远是。
那么何处是事件私下的转折，
那后来注定繁荣的，像金色的钟声
从一个最高的塔上传遍城市上空？
那发生在我身上的离奇事情，而且我告诉你，
你立刻明白我是什么意思？
什么由蜿蜒的道路抵达的果园
藏起它们？这些根在哪里？

是肿块和尝试
告诉我们是否会出名
我们的命运是否可以成为榜样，像一颗星辰。
余下的是等待
一封永远不会寄到的信，
日复一日，恼怒

直到最终你不知道它是什么撕开了它，

信封的两半放在一个盘子上。

内容是明智的，似乎

很久以前就口述了。

它的真理是永恒的，但它的时间

尚未到来，讲述危险，和通常有限的

可以抵御危险的步骤，

现在和未来，在凉爽的院子里。

在乡下安静的小房子里，

我们的乡下，在围着篱笆的区域，在凉爽背阴的街道。

第十交响曲

我还没告诉你
游艇展上痞子们的事。
但刚才看见游艇
在他们的卡车上驶过:
一片红色白色蓝色和红色
促使我去,想要挡住你的路。

很多事你从未和我讲过:
你为何爱我,我们为何爱你,到底
性是什么。当人们讨论它,
越来越多地,他们总是
在指牵扯到性器官的那种——
羞怯,含糊,难以想象,如同盲人眼中的它们?
我发现思考这些事情分裂我们,
把我们聚在一起。就像上次感恩节,
没人能吃完盘子里的菜,
然后表示感恩。对一些人
比对我意味着更多,我猜。
但我还是不确定。

有一些连接,
(我喜欢英国人拼写这个单词的方式
有些事情他们如此聪明
或许总的来说比我们精明
虽然应该有一些东西
我们有他们却没有——不要问我
它是什么。请不要谈开放。
我会选弗朗西斯·汤普森而非布雷塔·哈特
随时,如果我不得不)
在它们之间。它连接,
并非连向什么,而是类似于
让队伍抱团,以便使它们开放。
你可以"停车购物"。自助服务
和荣誉制度占了上风,导致
产生大量的业余时间,
对一些有益,对其他人更多是问题,
只是指出要绕道而行。
今天下午坐在客厅里我看见了
如何使用它。很久以前,我的幻景
依旧蚀刻在米黄色的墙上,一只选择性的
柴郡猫。无法取消,
消息是倒数第二个收到的。

所以过去这么多年,
略作闲游,
稍加放松,一堆计划和想法。
希望在可预见的未来,关于最后一个
有更多的时间告诉你。

在秋湖上

对树孽囔读骚烂取缔法是秋湖
这里的中国贤哲深思熟虑插入魁北克醒的
活动——闭嘴！我才不！边缘用愈加
家长作风的固执拥抱着湖，它的效果
在前方蓝蓝的上空。坐飞机

从其它地方到这里的距离不远，但
它不算数，至少不像海岸距离
那样——叶子，树，石头；选项（蕨类，青蛙，臭鼬）；
然后石头，树，叶子；然后另一个选项——算数。
它就像十九世纪学院派的"机械绘画"。
结果是你不需要所有这些训练
从事艺术——没有训练甚至更好。看看
印象派画家们——他们中一些也有，但宁愿忘记它
在巨大平静的画布上，色彩时而放纵
时而贫乏，缺乏的只是空间概念。

我认为这不会是
我最后一次去秋湖旅行

在许多严肃的头脑中交一些朋友
我们所有学者们都坐在树下
等待坚果落下。我们一些人学习
波斯语和阿拉姆语,其他人学习蒸馏术,
从虚无中提取怪异的香气,都是从零起步。
每一位都发挥了潜力,两条电线
在交叉。

对死亡的恐惧

我现在怎么了?
是否我已经变成了这样?
难道不存在没有以前和以后
边界线的状态? 今天窗户开着

空气穿着裙子,带着钢琴声
涌进来,仿佛要说:"看,约翰,
我带来了这些还有这些"——即
少许贝多芬,一些勃拉姆斯,

少许优选的普朗克音符……是的,
它又自由了,这空气,它必须不断回来
因为它的好处就是这些。
我想和它待在一起,因为恐惧

让我无法走上某些台阶,
敲某些门,害怕独自
老去,在小径黄昏的尽头
没看见任何人,除了另一个自己

点头打个招呼:"你已经有一段时间了,
但现在我们重归于好,这才是最重要的。"
我路上的空气,你可以缩短这个,
但微风已经减弱,沉默是最后的文字。

比尔颂

我们做的一些事情占用了更多时间
被认为是一件富有成效、自然的事情。
我要从一种行为方式出来,
进入一片犁过的玉米地。我的左边,海鸥们,
在内陆度假。它们似乎介意我的写作方式。

或者,换一个例子:上个月,
我发誓要写得更多。什么是写作?
这个,对我来说,是在纸上写下,
确切地说,不是思想,而是想法,也许:
关于思想的想法。思想是一个太宏大的词,
想法更好,虽然不完全是我的意思。
有一天我会解释。但不是今天。

我感觉好像有人给我做了件背心,
我在乡下的户外穿着它,
出于对那个人的忠诚,虽然
没有人看见,除了我自己
以及在内心中看见自己是什么样。

穿上它既是一项义务又是一种荣幸，
因为它吸收我，吸收我太多。

一匹马不规则地站立，引人注目，
衬着远方的大地。是我在接收
这片景象吗？它是我的吗？或者我已经亏欠了它，
为了其它景象，在时间巨大
松弛的曲线上未被注意，未被记录，
所有被遗忘的春天，落下的鹅卵石，
曾经听见然后放到光线之外的歌曲，
进入每天的遗忘中？他缓缓离去，
仰起头，向天空喷射一个久久不散去的
问题。连他我们也能为了最终的
进步牺牲，因为我们必须，我们必须继续前行。

立陶宛舞乐队

《智者纳旦》是一个好标题它重新引入
重杂质它们用拨动开关连接到一个个长环上
长环从文学和生活进入世间的混乱我们两个
没有工作的灵魂在里面挣扎因为回到总和
是一条漫漫长路与此同时我们生活在其中"渐渐
　适应了"
一切而且这个凌驾在生活之上并重叠在它上面
如同当一头受伤的豺狼被捆在水坑狮子真的来了

我给你写信表达这些个想法感情你极有
可能正驾驶着你的小车绕城转悠
呼吸进城市精致的空气和废气灰尘其它
构成它的东西请稍等会有时间
去做别的决定但现在我想要专注在你
这个安稳投射出的形象上我如何想象你
因为你就是那个样子你在何方你在我的脑海里

我身体里的某样东西受损我不知道怎么回事或
　因何而致

今天突然开阔整个不确定的时代正在结束
像第一次世界大战或二十年代它在不停结束这是后来
音乐的开始而小吃各种简单的美味
暖心并创造了一种热情洋溢的气氛与我们
内心中保持的那个正式的气氛相匹敌

天空中似乎挤满了这么多摩天大楼和飞艇和气球
　又如何
至少是一个生活不错的地方我觉得你意下如何
那里响起的歌声是合唱每个地方如此动听它是
　美好的
每个地方真理涌进来填补它突然消亡
留下的空隙以至于相当准确地记录它的活动是可能的
假如友谊中存在着性这个地板正是享用它的地方
钟声荡漾喧闹的音乐震耳欲聋

也许改天人们想要回顾这一切
因为今天它看上去像挤在一起的线条压缩
在其中一幅画面中你为了达到完整效果用一根
擦亮的管子反射出它们而这是可能的
我在气候贫乏的地带和呼啸着刮过
这些单调的街道的风中感受到它
把一切带到一个高光时刻

然而我们也是孑然一身这很悲哀不是吗
然而你就打算孑然一身至少一部分时间
你为了工作必须如此而它好像总是如此不自然
仿佛与人们见面是生活内在的东西或许就是如此
那么不知为何孤独是更真实更人性的
你不仅了解稻草人还了解整个风景
还有耙子犁过的地方那些平静地啄食的乌鸦

沙桶

红色
条纹穿过环保抽奖
大量冲刷的过程曲解了
涌现出来的厚板。一个
脚印
随着暴风雨在这种新情况下
向内弯曲，在平坦的番红花
广场中心指挥交通。为什么
还有发展？
一把透明的铁铲铺路，"它们"说，
残余的弹性镱铐，
瞬间的照片
埋在沙子下面。

无从知晓

然后呢？颜色和颜色的名字，
某种颜色曾经对你的了解？
整个歌包，嗡姆吧声副歌？
街景？骑自行车的人们过去后
模糊的路面？他们彼此呼叫，
他们管彼此叫奇怪的听上去滑稽的名字？
也许是的，但与此同时，在一个
梦的中间醒来，满嘴是
不认识的单词，包括了以下所有：
既表面，又是给那个表面造成
创伤的意外事故，但它也只包含
如同一本关于瑞典的书只包含那本书的页面。
阴冷的无何有之乡和虚幻的顶峰——
都在一次洪水的表面上飘飘然，
洪水什么也不在乎，
甚至不在乎管好自己的事。
过去我们曾经把节假日
搭配到一起，是的，它们是完美的
组合，但其它的日子发出臭味，

消耗它们的物质,变成孤儿,剥夺继承权,
但空气在帘子中站立,君临
如一场百年纪念。没人能进去和出来。
这些是同一个身体的一部分:
没有其中一些一个人或许也能活着
比如一根手指或肘部,但脑袋
是必需的,并且是这里起疑的。今天
上午它去上法语课了。
现在它在休息,不能被打扰。

是的,但是——不存在"是的,但是"。
身体是这所有的一切,它散开,
一层层碎片,全散落在某个地方,
但很难正确地解读,因为不存在
共同的制高点,不存在小说中
"我"这样的视角,而事实上,
没人看到其中任何一点。目击纱窗
愤怒地移动匆匆回到林子的边缘,
并默默地垂下眼睑,这如同
一片残茬地,里面永远存活着它自己
僵硬的二进制,从对真相的匮乏
了解中诱导出真相。它已经起作用
而且会继续起作用。所有影响这作用的

尝试是平行性，起伏，有时候
扭动，但被保留在隐喻的范畴。
无从知晓的是，这些是否是
我们的邻里，还是友好的野蛮人
被海市蜃楼的繁文缛节困在了远方。今天
早上我们只是懒散地对他们慢吞吞打招呼
并不意味着开创了一种风格。反正傍晚
对事情有所改变。与其说是颜色，
一次握手的质量，某人呼吸的锋芒，
不如说是一种普遍的焦虑，要把一切加起来，
花插好，在视野以外。载体的疯狂
继续，撞击，翻腾，但是
对许多人，这是几近尾声：一个人
可以把椅子拉近到阳台栏杆边。
夕阳正好开始放出光彩。

至于歌声何时开始响起，
能做的并不是很多。在香草
走廊里等待一位严厉的
年轻护士出现，一只胳膊上托着装在磨砂
玻璃花瓶里的金鱼草，女主角弱不禁风，
另一只放在背后下腰，这也拯救不了在死亡
香水中已经浸泡过的结局。乘客们

重现。抄近路的司机把他们推向天堂。

(沃特福德在石板上爆炸。)

同时,我们正在努力拼写出

这个非常简单的字,一个接一个地

放好音符,推回死翘翘的混乱,

它迂回在背景中,如同迷雾

笼罩欢快的秋野——你的钱死翘翘了。

而我喜欢这些歌曲的精神,

同志友情,那最后剥落的东西,

即使现在还能在树枝和暮色交织的

图案上看得见。你为何一定要走?你为何不能

留下来过夜,在我的床上,让我紧紧拥抱着你?

无疑,这会解决一切问题,通过用我们

保留的庞大的七零八碎的知识,

在一定规模上提供一个知识理论:

一张你所有心爱的友情的黑胶唱片,

前线来信?太

神奇了,说不通。但它让钟声响起。

如果你去听,你能听见钟声依旧回荡:

一种情绪,一种气氛,汇总成一种关于它们曾经
  为何物的感觉,

一直在穿过一连串日益变长的白天。

套房

惰性的无生命的块状向空间里面呼喊：
漫长的七年，墙尚未修建，
外壳变厚，一切的背面……
簇集的排钟和事后的想法那粉红的露水
支撑它。

这本应要被忘却，从历史中
清除。但时间是一座花园，记忆
在里面可怕地茁壮成长，直到
它们成为另一样东西漂泊开花，
如同带着你的雨衣停在栅栏附近。

在夜里，橙色的迷雾。
太阳已经杀死一万亿个它们，
而且它不停地向后延伸，不可能的行星。
我怎么知道？我迷失了。它说出它的名字。
花园尽头蓝黑色的信息
被篡改了。与此同时，我们应该在这里，
在松林里呼吸美好的新鲜空气。

雪是他最不期待的东西。
太阳，它的吻，陌生的土地，
刺耳的口音却奇怪地友善，
现在从解开纽扣的角落搬出去，
出来，这一天推迟的演出。
难以置信。它真正让你了解你自己。
这一天完整了，眼睛和报告一起，寂静。

童话图画

从前……不,它太沉重了
没法说。还有,你也不再用心听。
我该怎么说呢?
"雨轰隆隆地砸在红色的石板上。

坚定的锡兵透过大雨凝视着远方,
回想起那帽子形状的纸船,那么快……"
也不是这样。
想想过去夏天漫长的傍晚,野胡萝卜花。

有时,一个乐句会完美地概括
一个瞬间的情绪。那些为管乐器而做的失恋
奏鸣曲中的一首正骑着庄严的白马过去。
每个人都在琢磨那新来者是谁。

花团锦簇,第二天被丢弃的
装饰品。现在看看窗外吧。
天空清澈沉闷。错误的一天
不管谈生意还是游戏,或为一件确定的事打赌。

树木在夜里哭泣,把雨滴
流进水里。恋人们慢慢聚到一起。
她望着他的双眼。"一个人独处
感觉不会好。"他:"我会留下来

只要夜晚允许。"这是那些彩色负片的
夜晚彩虹中的一个。我们向前,它后退;我们看见
自己现在进到洞穴深处,必须是。但那里好像
到处是树,一阵风拂动树叶,轻轻地。

我想回去,摆脱糟糕的故事,
但永远有一种可能,下一个是……
不,它是另一棵杏树,或一只咽下戒指的青蛙……
而它们是美丽的,随着我们用自己

把它们填满。它们空如衣柜。
每天完全浸泡在里面,等待下一次低语,
隔壁下一个字。这就是王子们一定的表现,
在睡眠的节俭中躺下。

城市下午

一层烟雾保护着这张
照片里每个人已经忘记的这个很久
以前的下午,他们中大多数现在
很烂,尖叫着穿过老年和死亡。

假如一个人可以抓住美国
或至少是一种微小的遗忘,
它渗进我们的轮廓,
用一个同样稍纵即逝的污渍
界定我们的容量

但是纪念着,
因为它毕竟在界定:
灰色花环,那三人性爱
等待着光线发生变化,
空气撩拨一个人的头发,
他在倒影池中倒转。

罗宾汉的谷仓

就是这一天:几滴小雨,

这个少许,空气中一丝古龙水的味道,

只要它令人浮想联翩。而它

上升,一支小夜曲,到围拢的

爱。你们这些坏鸟,

但上帝不会惩罚你们,你们

会与我们同在天堂,虽然也许

不如我们意识到你们的幸福。

地狱大概不是相当令人满意的天堂,

但你们是我安排的

水果和珠宝:啊,和我在一起吧!

忘记冷漠,一丝不苟记下

严苛的条款!平庸的

太阳将在它每日的转动中

爬过天空:不要让它发现我们在争吵,

或更糟糕,独自地,每一位

已经背对着另一位,

独自在新的一天

奇妙的孤独里。在那里

不是去了解它,它的轮廓
爬着靠近你们,然后它已然落在你们上面
像雾的被褥。
从放在楼梯顶端附近
宁静的高桌那里,
彻底进入我们的
考虑,虽然它像柠檬水一样寡味。
余下的被梦见,如同潮湿的地面上
这场宴席的外壳。
当我在转身对她说什么时,她飞驰过我身边,
这意味着几年后一切结束:二十六,二十七,
那时候下船
来见我们的人是谁?
你们年轻的岁月成为一种陶土,
从中塑造更加古老、完善也更加
粗鲁的反驳,那带你们
进入夜晚的问候,
像一盏眼前的灯笼:
那些"你们曾在何方";与此同时
黑暗在等待,像如此多的其他东西,
比如沉默不语和骄奢淫逸。
成为它的一部分是好的,
在深植其中作为内核的

梦中,朴实无华,不脸红,
但也是伸向远方的陡峭的一面:
为这个我们付钱,为这个
在今夜和每一夜。
但暂时我们是自由的,
而与此同时,歌曲
保护我们,以某种方式,还有这特殊气候。

全部和一些

而且为那些明白的人:
我们移动了那一天,直到不再有什么
从我们如此模仿的情况中出来。
现在我们谈论它
不是作为一个人,彬彬有礼,聪明绝顶,
站出来谈论忧心忡忡的事情
而是作为对它自己有趣的描述而已。

因此所有的良好意图都是弱小的,
原样委托给了生命的血液
那冰冷的露水和烦人的气候。
阴沉的黎明是否会以旋花的图案悬垂,
第二天中午将它改变,暗淡,光秃秃,不悲惨,
直到图案开始显得仅仅像脚步,
干燥,快乐,溺爱老式的,每月一次的。

"气候"不是一个征兆,但它可以是
一个副产品,一个匿名的蓝领郊区
在巨大的温和中,这温和用折断的

轮齿和灵巧的倒转控制了气氛。
瞎子太阳开始为此事负责,
但与此同时房屋已经建好
实际上已有人入住了它的一部分。

但我的意思是不存在借口
可以总是从个别推断出普遍,
像那个太阳上的斑点。多少
无助的哀号穿过滑溜溜的舞池
退出管弦乐队,直到连那些
舞者也在那里,起初跛脚跳着华尔兹,
但现在一动不动,嗡嗡叫,像格子呢?再没有

人在乎或使用那个小车站。
他们太年轻了,不记得
晚班的火车进站时是什么情景。
紫罗兰色的天空在灰色的山顶上放牧。
何等懒惰的胃口
让秃鹰不停盘旋,当黎明到来,
它四轮驱动往上,没有借口或唧唧歪歪。

不可能描绘当时关系的
牢固。松弛部分

按照定义得到弥补,所以
一切都是有用的。人们死去,
为漫长的等待感到高兴,
往下午,往那些山丘吐出只言片语:
于是甜蜜最后一次被击倒。

你是否记得我们曾经采撷
那车叶草,那车叶草?但不是
所有东西都能得到颂扬,但许多
肯定可以,而那几位专心致志的
凭借心血来潮,摆脱时间之爪的
威严,过着快乐有用的生活,
没有意识到宇宙是一个巨大的孵化器。

清晰地感知到这个不是去了解它,哎——
今天各种方向来自于许多分开的领域,
在一个光秃秃的底座那里连成一体。
太多军队,太多梦,就这样吧。
再见,你说,直到下一次
而我营造我们的气候,直到下一次,
但天空皱眉,工作在一个梦中得到完成。

仁慈之油

把它擦掉,减少毒性,
同时也试着从头开始
重新安排整个事情。
是的我们刚才在等待
是的我们不再等待。

后来,当我告诉你
仿佛这一切只是作为
我的故事的侧线发生

我求你听我说
你已经在听

它已经把自己关在外面
这样做时,意外地把我们关在里面

与此同时,我的故事进展顺利
第一章
　　　告一段落

但真正的故事，他们

告诉我们我们也许永远不会知道的那个

断断续续飘回来

结果是，它们都

如此幸运

现在我们真的知道

一切都是偶然发生的：

一次邂逅

侏儒把你带到一条街的尽头

挥动手臂指着两个方向

你忘记了蔑视他

但是在一系列插曲发生

在带家具的房间里（描述墙纸）之后

临时酒店（提及水槽和蟑螂）

以及和一位美丽的已婚妇女共度良宵

她的丈夫出差去了森特维尔

（提及这墙纸：最纯洁的玫瑰

虽然是最凝脂的，她的

微笑如何减轻

最后五百页的折磨

虽然你从来不知道她的姓

只知道她的名字：多萝西）

你抓住了生命之水
拯救了你两个邪恶的兄弟卡什和杰思罗
他们及时偷走了生命之水
那之后你拿了回来,平安到家,
救了老头子的命
继承了王国。

但这一个时刻是
在最欢快的阳光下。
在更贫瘠的大地上
没有人碰生命之水。

它无味
虽然它绝对令人振作
它是一个还必须传递的杯子

直到每个人
获得某种或大或小的优势
某种理由,让他走得
如此远
不带狗和女人
如此远,独自一人,未请自行。

凸面镜中的自画像

如帕米贾尼诺所画,右手
比头还大,向观看者推去,
又轻易转开,仿佛要保护
它所展现的。几扇铅格窗玻璃,旧梁,
毛皮,带褶子的平纹细布,珊瑚戒指,
一起运行支撑面孔,面孔游
过来又游走,像那只手,
只不过它神色安然。它就是那
被隔开的。瓦萨里说,"弗朗西斯科有一天着手
画自己的肖像,为此他看着凸面镜里的
自己,就是理发师们用的那种……
他让木料旋工照着做了
一个木球,然后把它分成两半,
做成镜子的大小,着手
用高超的技艺临摹他在镜中看见的一切,"
主要是他的映像,其肖像
是那个映像又隔开一层。
镜面选择只映射他所看见的,
足以满足他的目的:他的形象

上了釉，经过防腐处理，以180度的角度投射。
白天的时间和附着于面孔的
光的强度，让它在反复
抵达的波浪中保持活泼，
完整。灵魂建立了自己。
但是通过眼睛它能游出去多远
然后仍然能安全返回巢穴？镜子的
表面是凸面，距离明显
增加；也就是，足以表明
灵魂是囚徒，得到人道待遇，被悬
在空中，无法超过你的目光
走得更远，当目光拦截住画面。
克莱门特教皇和他的教廷看到后
"惊呆了"，据瓦萨里说，而且承诺佣金
但永远没有兑付。灵魂不得不待在原地，
尽管焦躁不安，听见雨滴落在窗玻璃上，
外面，风抽打着秋天的树叶发出
叹息，渴望自由，但它必须摆好姿势
待在这个地方。它必须
尽可能少动。这是这幅肖像所说的。
但在这个凝视中，混杂着
柔情、喜悦和惋惜，如此用力
克制，以致人们无法长久地看着。

这秘密太明显了。它的怜悯恼人，
让热泪喷发：那灵魂不是一个灵魂。
没有秘密，小小的，而且它恰好
适合自己的空穴：它的房间，我们关注的时刻。
那是曲调，但没有词语。
词语仅仅是推测（speculation）
（来自于拉丁文 speculum，镜子）：
它们找寻，却无法发现音乐的含义。
我们只是看见梦的姿势，
移动的骑手们在傍晚的天空下
将这张面孔带入视野，没有
虚假的混乱作为真实性的证明。
但它是被锁进球体的生命。
一个人想要把手伸出
球体，但它的维度，
那承载它的，不会允许它。
无疑它就是这样，不是要隐藏
什么东西的反射体，它让那只手凸显，
随着它微微回撤。没有办法
把它建成扁平的，像一段墙：
它必须加入圆圈的一节，
漫游回身体，它看上去如此不像
其中一部分，它去围住，支撑起面孔，

这种情况在它上面的努力看上去
像一丝微笑,一个火花
或星星,当黑暗重临,一个人不确定
是否看见了。一束怪异的光,它
微妙的要求提前毁灭了它
想要闪亮的妙思:无足轻重却意欲如此。
弗朗西斯科,你的手足够大,
可以毁掉这个球体,而且太大了,
人们会想,它无法编织精致的网格,
它们只会主张进一步拘禁。
(大,但不粗糙,仅仅在另一个尺度上,
如同一头在海底打盹儿的鲸鱼,
相对于海面上那艘渺小
自以为是的轮船。)但你的眼睛宣告
一切都是表面。这表面是在那儿的
而除了在那儿的,没有什么能够存在。
房间里没有凹室,只有壁龛,
而窗户不怎么重要,还有那
窄条窗和右边的镜子,即使
作为一个气象计,它在法语中是
Le temps,表示时间,而且它
跟随一条线路,变化在其中仅仅是
整体的特征。整体在不稳定性中

是稳定的,一个球体,如同我们的,放在
真空的底座上,一个乒乓球
稳立在它喷射的水柱上。
正如没有词语表示表面,即,
没有词语描述它到底是什么,它不是
肤浅的,但是一个有形的核,那么就
没有办法解决移情和经验相对立的问题。
你会继续待下去,焦躁,在你的
姿态里宁静,既不是拥抱,又不是警告,
但它在什么也不肯定的纯粹
肯定中拥有某种两者都是的东西。

气球爆裂,注意力
无精打采地转开。水坑里的
云涌动,散落成锯齿形的碎片。
我想到来看过
我的朋友们,想到昨天是
什么样子。一道记忆特殊的
斜光在寂静的画室里侵扰
那个梦中的模特,随着他考虑着
举起画笔画自画像。
多少人来过,待了一段时间,
说出的轻松或沉重的话语,成为你的一部分,

如同风吹起的雾和沙子后面的光线,
被它过滤和影响,直到没有任何部分
留下来确定是你。那些黄昏里的声音
已经告诉你一切,然而故事依旧继续
以记忆的形式储存在不规则的
水晶堆里。谁弯曲的手在控制,
弗朗西斯科,四季轮转和那些想法,
它们气喘吁吁地剥落,飞走,
如同那些最后的倔强的树叶从湿漉漉的
枝条上被撕掉?我在这个里面只看见你
圆镜子的混乱,它围绕着你一双眼睛的
准星组织一切,你的眼睛是空的,
一无所知,做着梦,但一无所示。
我感觉到旋转木马在慢慢启动,
然后越来越快:书桌,报纸,书籍,
朋友们的照片,窗户和树木,
在一条中立带里面融合,从四周
包围我,不管我看向哪里。
而我无法解释流平的行为,
为何一切应该都归结为一种
统一的物质,一种内部的岩浆。
我在这些事情上的向导是你的自我,
坚定,间接,用同样幽灵般的微笑

接受一切,并随着时间加速,它立刻
晚了很多,我只能知道直接出去的路,
我们之间的距离。很久以前,
散落的证据意味着什么,
随着白天笨拙地前行,
它的小事故和快乐,
一个家庭主妇做着家务。现在完全不可能
在银色的模糊中恢复那些特性,那模糊
记录了你坐下,"用高超的技艺临摹你
在镜中看见的一切"所完成的,
为了永远完善和排除那些
无关的。在你各种意图的圆圈里某些翼梁
保留,延续自我对自我的陶醉:
目光,平纹细布,珊瑚。这不重要
因为这些是今天依旧如此的东西,
在一个人的影子伸展出田野
进入明天的想法之前。

明天是容易的,但今天尚未绘制,
荒凉,像任何风景一样不情愿
产生透视法的内容,
毕竟只是对画家深深
不信任,一种虽然必要却微弱的

工具。当然，一些东西

是可能的，它知道，但它不知道

是哪些。总有一天，我们会尝试

去做尽可能多的事情

也许我们将成功做到其中

一些，但这个不会和今天

所许诺的有任何关系，我们的

风景席卷着离开我们，消失

在天边。今天，足够的外罩磨光

把各种假设的许诺保持

在一片表面上，让人们从它们那里

闲逛回家，为了让这些

更强大的可能性能够无需测试

而保持完整。实际上，

气泡室的外壳坚硬

如爬行动物的蛋；在适当的时候，一切在那里

"程序化"了：不断有更多的被包括进来

却没有增加总数，正如一个人

开始习惯了一种噪声，它

让他保持清醒，但已然不复如此，

房间包含了这种流动，如同一个沙漏

没有在气候或特征上发生变化

（也许除了在一个向着死亡聚拢的焦点上

发出凄冷几乎看不见的光亮——后来
愈发如此）。应该是一个梦的真空
不断地变得充盈，随着梦的源头
被开发，因此这一个梦
也许会丰满，像一朵卷心菜玫瑰盛开，
蔑视反奢侈法令，让我们
醒来，试着开始生活在现在已经
成为贫民窟的地方。西德尼·弗里德伯格在他的
《帕米贾尼诺》中关于它说道："这幅肖像里的现实
　主义
不再产生一种客观的真实，而是一种怪异……
然而它的变形并没有产生
一种不和谐的感觉……形式严格
遵循一种理想美的尺度"，因为
靠我们的梦滋养，如此微不足道，直到有一天
我们注意到它们留下来的洞。现在它们的重要性，
如果不是它们的意义，显而易见。它们是要滋养
一个包括它们全部的梦，因为它们
在聚积的镜中始终是反转的。
它们看上去奇怪，因为我们实际上看不见它们。
而我们只是在它们消失的那个点上才意识到这个，
如同浪击碎在岩石上，用一个表达
自己的形状的姿势放弃了那个形状。

形式严格遵循理想美的尺度

随着它们秘密搜寻着我们变形的想法。

何必因为这种安排不开心,既然

梦被吸收的时候延长了我们?

某种像活着的事情发生,一种运动

离开梦,进入它的法典。

随着我开始忘记它,

它的陈腐模式再次出现,

但它是一种不熟悉的陈腐模式,那张面孔

停泊妥当,来自各种危险,很快

和其他人搭讪,"与其说是人,不如说是天使"(瓦萨里)。

也许一位天使看上去像我们

已经忘记的一切。我的意思是忘记的

事物,似乎不熟悉了,当我们再次

遇见它们,无法言喻地迷茫,

它们曾经是我们的。这会是侵犯

这个人的隐私的意义,他

"涉猎过炼金术,但他此处的

愿望不是以抽离的科学精神

来审视艺术的微妙之处;他希望通过

它们给予观看者新奇和惊异感"

（弗里德伯格）。后期肖像，比如乌菲齐的
《绅士》、波格赛的《年轻教士》和
那不勒斯的《安提亚》，源自矫饰主义的
张力，但在这里，正如弗里德伯格指出，
那惊叹，那张力是在概念中，
而不是在它的实现中。
文艺复兴盛期的和谐
出现了，虽然被镜子扭曲了。
新颖的是在展现圆形反射面的
微妙倾斜度时所投入的极致用心，
（它是第一幅镜面肖像），
以至有一片刻你被愚弄了，
然后你意识到镜中映像
不是你的。你那时感觉就像那些霍夫曼
笔下人物中的一个，已经被剥夺了
镜子映像，除了看见我的整体
被画家在他的其它
房间里那严格的他性
所取代。我们已经让工作中的他
大吃一惊，但是不，他工作时
已经让我们大吃一惊。那幅画快完成了，
惊讶也快过去，如同当一个人往外看，
一个雪球吓了他一跳，就是现在，雪球

正结束在亮晶晶的雪粒中。
它发生了,当你在屋里,睡着了,
不存在什么理由,你应该
为它醒着,除了那白天
正在结束,而今夜你会很难
入睡,至少要到深夜。

城市的阴影注入它自己的
紧迫性:罗马,大洗劫期间
弗朗西斯科在那里工作:他的发明
让朝他闯进来的士兵感到惊奇;
他们决定饶了他的命,而他很快就离开了;
维也纳,如今那幅画在那里,1959 年
夏天我和皮埃尔在那儿看到它;纽约,
我现在所在的地方,它是
其他城市的对数。我们的风景
充满各种起源,穿梭来往;
生意运作是靠表情、手势
和道听途说。对这座城市,它是另一种生活,
不能辨认但精确描绘的画室里
那面镜子的背衬。它想要
吸走画室的生活,把它绘制的
空间压瘪成法规条文,孤立起来。

这次行动已经暂停

但某种新的事物正在路上,风中

一种新的故作风雅。你能承受它吗

弗朗西斯科?你足够强大对付它吗?

这阵风带来它所不知的,自我

推进,盲目,没有任何自我

概念。正是惰性,一旦

得到承认,消弱了所有的活动,秘密或公开:

小声说着无法理解但可以

感受到的词语,一阵寒意,一种枯萎病

沿着你叶脉的海岬和半岛

向外扩散,并如此向着群岛,

然后向着公海沐风栉雨的秘密。

这是它的负面。它的正面是

让你注意到生活,还有只是看上去

在消失的压力,但现在,

随着这个新的模式提出疑问,人们看见它们

匆匆忙忙摆脱时尚。如果它们打算成为经典,

它们必须决定站在哪一边。

它们的缄默已经瓦解了

城市场景,使它的模棱两可

看上去任性又倦乏,一个老人的游戏。

我们现在需要的是这位难以相信的

挑战者在撞击一座受惊的城堡的
大门。你的论点,弗朗西斯科,
开始变得不再新鲜,因为见不到
任何前来应答的影子。如果它现在
化为尘土,那只是意味着它的时间
不久前已经到来,但现在去看,去听:
也许是另一个生命储存在那里,
在无人知晓的凹室里;也许是它,
不是我们,是这个变化;也许我们实际上是它,
倘若我们可以回到它,重新感受一些它
看上去的样子,将我们的脸转向放稳的球体,
然后仍然能一切安然无恙:
神经正常,呼吸正常。既然它是一个比喻
用来包括我们,我们是它的一部分,而且
能在它里面生活,正如实际上我们已然如此,
只是让我们的思想裸着,因为质疑,
我们现在发现,不会随意发生,
而是井然有序,这意味着不威胁
任何人——事情完成的正常方式,
如同围绕着生命从日子中生长出的
同心力:准确无误地,如果你仔细想想。

一阵微风,像一页书翻过去,

带回你的面孔:这个时刻

咬了这么大一口它所追求的

愉悦的直觉的迷雾。

这锁定到位是"死亡本身",

如同贝尔格提到的马勒第九中的一个乐句;

或者,引用《辛白林》里伊摩琴的话:"死亡的

痛苦也不会比这更让人难受,"因为,

虽然仅仅是练习或策略,它

携带着一个正在建立的信念的动能。

仅仅遗忘无法移除它,

企盼也无法唤回它,只要它依旧是

自己的梦的白色沉淀,

在叹息的气候中,那叹息横贯我们的世界

如同鸟笼的罩布。但确定的是

美丽的事物只有与一个具体的生命相关时似乎

才美丽,无论经历与否,被引导进某种形式,

沉浸于对一个共同的过去的缅怀中。

光线今天带着一种热情暗下来,

我曾在别的地方见过,并且知道为何

它似乎是有意义的,知道别人多年前

也有同样的感受。我继续咨询

这面不再是我的镜子,

因为这一次我的部分如同

活跃的真空。而花瓶总是满的

因为只有这么多空间

而且它容纳了一切。人们

看见的样本不会仅仅

被当作那个,而是作为一切,如同它

在时间外可以被想象的那样——不是作为一个姿势,

而是作为全部,在精致的可同化的状态中。

但是这个宇宙是什么的门廊

随着它转进转出,向前又退后,

拒绝包围我们,又仍然是我们唯一

能看见的东西?爱曾经

倾斜了天平,但现在笼罩在阴影下,看不见,

虽然神秘地存在,在某个地方附近。

但我们知道它不可能被夹在

两个相邻的时刻中间,它蜿蜒曲折

不通往任何地方,除了朝着更远的支流

而它们将自己注入一个对某样

东西模糊的感觉中,人们永远无法了解它,

尽管我们每一个人似乎都有可能

了解它是什么,并有能力

把它传递给对方。但一些人

作为一个标志表现出的样子让人想要

往前推进,忽视那种尝试

表面的天真，不在乎
没人在倾听，既然那光
在他们的眼中永远地点燃，
它存在，完好无损，一件永久的异常事物，
清醒，无声。在它的表面上
似乎没有特殊原因，那个光为何
应该被爱所聚焦，或者为何
城市带着它美丽的郊区一起沉沦
落入永远更加不清晰更加不明确的空间，
应该解读为对它的进步的支持，
一个画架，戏剧在上面展开，
朝着自我满足，朝着我们
梦幻的尽头，因为我们从未想象过
它会终结，在残破的日光中，描绘出的
承诺投射过来，仿佛一种抵押物，一种债券。
这没有特征的、难以界定的白昼是
它在那里发生的秘密，
我们无法再回到收集起来的
相互冲突的不同观点，主要见证人
记忆的失误。我们所知道的
是我们有点早了，而
今天有那种特殊的、切割磨光的
今天性，阳光把细枝影子投射

在漫不经心的人行道上时

将它忠实地复制。前面没有一个日子会像这样。

我曾经以为它们一模一样，

以为当下在每个人眼中总是一样的。

但这种混乱消失，当一个人

总是在他的当下中达到顶峰。

而带回到那幅画的长长的走廊

"诗意的"麦秆色空间，

它正在变暗的反面——这个是不是

"艺术"的某种虚构，并不是要想象成

真实的，更不用说是特殊的？它不是在当下中

也有一个巢穴，我们一直在逃脱，

又跌入，如同日子的水车

遵循着自己平淡无奇，甚至平静的轨迹？

我认为它是想说就是今天，

我们必须离开它，即使公众

现在正拥挤着穿过博物馆，为了

在闭馆前离开。你无法住在那里。

过去灰色的釉彩攻击一切专门知识：

要用毕生学习的清洗抛光的

秘密，降低到一本书中

黑白插图的地位，那里彩板

极罕见。也就是，所有时间

没有降低到任何特殊的时间。没有人
提及那变化；这么做或许会
把注意力引到自己身上
那会增加担忧，害怕看完
整个藏品前出不去
（除了地下室的雕塑，
它们本来就属于那个地方）。
我们的时间因画像忍耐的意志
得到妥协，被遮掩起来。它暗示了
我们自己的意志，我们希望隐藏起来。
我们不需要绘画和成熟的
诗人们写的打油诗，当
爆炸如此精确，如此细微。
甚至承认所有这一切的存在
是否还有任何意义？它确实
存在吗？无疑，不再存在
闲暇时间沉迷于庄重的
消遣。今天没有边缘，事件带着
锋芒涌入，由同一种物质构成，
无法区分。"游戏"是别的东西：
它存在，在一个专门为了表达
自己而组织起来的社会里。
没有其它方式，那些混蛋，

想把一切都和他们的镜像游戏混为一谈，
似乎会增加赌注和可能性，或者
至少在模糊不清的压抑的嘲弄中
通过一种乔装的气质侵蚀
整体建筑来混淆问题，
他们完全离题了。他们被淘汰出局，
而游戏比赛并不存在，直到他们被淘汰。
它似乎是一个非常充满敌意的宇宙，
但是，因为每一个独特的东西对所有
其他的东西是敌意的，并以它们为代价存在，
如哲学家们经常指出的那样，至少
这个东西，这个无声的、没有分割的当下，
具有逻辑上的正当性，它
在这种情况下不是一件坏事情，
也不会是，如果讲诉的方式
不会以某种方式干扰，将最终结果扭曲成
一幅自身的漫画。这总是
发生，如同在游戏比赛中，
低声说的一个短语在屋子里传递，
最后变成完全不一样的东西。
正是这原则让艺术作品与艺术家的
初衷如此不同。经常，他发现
他已经省略了一开始自己打算说的

那个东西。被鲜花,外在的
欢愉诱惑,他责怪自己(虽然
私下里对结果满意),想象
他对这件事有发言权,做出了
自己几乎没有意识到的一个选择,
不知道是必要性绕过了这些解决方案
以便为它自己创造出某种
新东西,不知道没有其他方式,
不知道创造的历史是根据严格的规律
进展的,并且事情是
以这种方式得以完成,但永远不是那些
我们着手去完成,并强烈地想要
看见它们形成的东西。帕米贾尼诺
一定意识到了这点,当他致力于他的
阻挡生命的任务。人们被迫将顺利
或许甚至乏味(但如此神秘)的
完成解读为完美可行地
达成了一个目的。还有什么值得
严肃对待,在这种他性之外,
在日常活动最普通的形式里
包含了他性,轻微又深刻地
改变了一切,把创造,任何创造
这件事,也不仅仅是艺术创造,从我们

手中夺走，置之于附近某个恐怖的
顶峰，太近了无法忽视，太远了
无人能干预？这个他性，这个
"不是-作为-我们"是镜子中唯一
可看的，虽然没人可以说清
它何以变成这样。一艘飘着
陌生旗帜的船已进入了港湾。
你正在允许不相关的事情
拆散你的日子，模糊水晶球的
焦点。它的景色飘走
如水蒸汽四散在风中。丰富的
思绪联翩，以前如此轻易地
产生，现在不复，或极少出现。它们的
色彩没那么强烈，经过秋天的
风雨洗刷，破损，污浊，
还给了你，因为它们不值一文。
而我们是这样的习惯性生物，以至于
它们的含义永久存在，混淆
问题。只是严肃地对待性
也许是一种方式，但沙子发出沙沙声，
当它们接近巨大的滑落的开始，
进入所发生的事情。这个过去
现在在这里：画家

映照出的面孔,我们徜徉其中,
在未指定的频率上接收梦
和灵感,但色泽已经变得像金属,
曲线和边沿并不很丰富。每个人
都有一个大理论来解释宇宙,
但它没有讲述整个故事,
最终,重要是在他外面的
东西,对他,尤其是对我们,
我们尚未得到任何帮助
来破解自己真人大小的商,
必须依赖于二手知识。而我知道
其他任何人的品味都不会
有何帮助,可以不妨忽略。
它曾经是如此完美——细腻的带雀斑的
皮肤上的光泽,嘴唇湿润,仿佛要张开,
发表演讲,人们忘记的衣服
和家具那熟悉的样子。
这个可能是完美的天堂:在一个疲惫的
世界里异域风情的避难所,但那不可能
发生,因为它不可能是
重点。模仿自然状态也许是获得
一种内心宁静的第一步,
但它也仅仅是第一步,而且经常

保持着一个冻僵的欢迎姿势,在它
后面出现的空气里被蚀刻,
一种惯例。我们真的
没有时间给这些,除了用它们
来点火。它们越快燃烧干净,
对我们不得不扮演的角色越好。
因此我恳求你,撤回那只手,
不再伸出来当做盾牌或问候,
一种问候的盾牌,弗朗西斯科:
房间里还有一颗子弹的空间:
我们透过望远镜错误的一端
观看,当你后退的速度
比光线还快,最终在房间的
特征中变成扁平,一封永远
没有寄出的邀请函,那个"一切皆梦"
综合征,虽然"一切"足够简洁地
讲述它如何并非如此。它的存在
是真实的,虽然受到困扰,而这个
醒着的梦的疼痛永远无法淹没
依旧画在风中的简图,
它是为我选的,对我有意义,显现
在我房间里掩饰一切的光辉中。
我们已看见了这座城市;它是一只虫子

凸出的镜中之眼。所有事情都发生
在它的阳台上,并在那里继续,
但行动是一次盛会冰冷、糖浆般的
流动。人们感到太受限制,
筛着四月的阳光寻找线索,
在它的参数从容不迫的纯粹的
静止中。那只手没拿粉笔,
整体的每一部分都在脱落,
无法知道它曾经知道,除了
这里和那里,在回忆冰冷的
口袋里,来自时间的低语。

**SELF-PORTRAIT
IN A
CONVEX MIRROR**

As One Put Drunk into the Packet-Boat

I tried each thing, only some were immortal and free.

Elsewhere we are as sitting in a place where sunlight

Filters down, a little at a time,

Waiting for someone to come. Harsh words are spoken,

As the sun yellows the green of the maple tree. . . .

So this was all, but obscurely

I felt the stirrings of new breath in the pages

Which all winter long had smelled like an old catalogue.

New sentences were starting up. But the summer

Was well along, not yet past the mid-point

But full and dark with the promise of that fullness,

That time when one can no longer wander away

And even the least attentive fall silent

To watch the thing that is prepared to happen.

A look of glass stops you

And you walk on shaken: was I the perceived?

Did they notice me, this time, as I am,

Or is it postponed again? The children
Still at their games, clouds that arise with a swift
Impatience in the afternoon sky, then dissipate
As limpid, dense twilight comes.
Only in that tooting of a horn
Down there, for a moment, I thought
The great, formal affair was beginning, orchestrated,
Its colors concentrated in a glance, a ballade
That takes in the whole world, now, but lightly,
Still lightly, but with wide authority and tact.

The prevalence of those gray flakes falling?
They are sun motes. You have slept in the sun
Longer than the sphinx, and are none the wiser for it.
Come in. And I thought a shadow fell across the door
But it was only her come to ask once more
If I was coming in, and not to hurry in case I wasn't.

The night sheen takes over. A moon of cistercian pallor
Has climbed to the center of heaven, installed,
Finally involved with the business of darkness.
And a sigh heaves from all the small things on earth,
The books, the papers, the old garters and union-suit buttons

Kept in a white cardboard box somewhere, and all the lower

Versions of cities flattened under the equalizing night.

The summer demands and takes away too much,

But night, the reserved, the reticent, gives more than it takes.

Worsening Situation

Like a rainstorm, he said, the braided colors
Wash over me and are no help. Or like one
At a feast who eats not, for he cannot choose
From among the smoking dishes. This severed hand
Stands for life, and wander as it will,
East or west, north or south, it is ever
A stranger who walks beside me. O seasons,
Booths, chaleur, dark-hatted charlatans
On the outskirts of some rural fete,
The name you drop and never say is mine, mine!
Some day I'll claim to you how all used up
I am because of you but in the meantime the ride
Continues. Everyone is along for the ride,
It seems. Besides, what else is there?
The annual games? True, there are occasions
For white uniforms and a special language
Kept secret from the others. The limes
Are duly sliced. I know all this
But can't seem to keep it from affecting me,

Every day, all day. I've tried recreation,

Reading until late at night, train rides

And romance.

                        One day a man called while I was out

And left this message: "You got the whole thing wrong

From start to finish. Luckily, there's still time

To correct the situation, but you must act fast.

See me at your earliest convenience. And please

Tell no one of this. Much besides your life depends on it."

I thought nothing of it at the time. Lately

I've been looking at old-fashioned plaids, fingering

Starched white collars, wondering whether there's a way

To get them really white again. My wife

Thinks I'm in Oslo—Oslo, France, that is.

Forties Flick

The shadow of the Venetian blind on the painted wall,
Shadows of the snake-plant and cacti, the plaster animals,
Focus the tragic melancholy of the bright stare
Into nowhere, a hole like the black holes in space.
In bra and panties she sidles to the window:
Zip! Up with the blind. A fragile street scene offers itself,
With wafer-thin pedestrians who know where they are going.
The blind comes down slowly, the slats are slowly tilted up.

Why must it always end this way?
A dais with woman reading, with the ruckus of her hair
And all that is unsaid about her pulling us back to her, with her
Into the silence that night alone can't explain.
Silence of the library, of the telephone with its pad,
But we didn't have to reinvent these either:
They had gone away into the plot of a story,
The "art" part— knowing what important details to leave out
And the way character is developed. Things too real
To be of much concern, hence artificial, yet now all over

    the page,

The indoors with the outside becoming part of you

As you find you had never left off laughing at death,

The background, dark vine at the edge of the porch.

As You Came from the Holy Land

of western New York state

were the graves all right in their bushings

was there a note of panic in the late August air

because the old man had peed in his pants again

was there turning away from the late afternoon glare

as though it too could be wished away

was any of this present

and how could this be

the magic solution to what you are in now

whatever has held you motionless

like this so long through the dark season

until now the women come out in navy blue

and the worms come out of the compost to die

it is the end of any season

you reading there so accurately

sitting not wanting to be disturbed

as you came from that holy land

what other signs of earth's dependency were upon you

what fixed sign at the crossroads

what lethargy in the avenues

where all is said in a whisper

what tone of voice among the hedges

what tone under the apple trees

the numbered land stretches away

and your house is built in tomorrow

but surely not before the examination

of what is right and will befall

not before the census

and the writing down of names

remember you are free to wander away

as from other times other scenes that were taking place

the history of someone who came too late

the time is ripe now and the adage

is hatching as the seasons change and tremble

it is finally as though that thing of monstrous interest

were happening in the sky

but the sun is setting and prevents you from seeing it

out of night the token emerges

its leaves like birds alighting all at once under a tree

taken up and shaken again

put down in weak rage

knowing as the brain does it can never come about

not here not yesterday in the past

only in the gap of today filling itself

as emptiness is distributed

in the idea of what time it is

when that time is already past

A Man of Words

His case inspires interest

But little sympathy; it is smaller

Than at first appeared. Does the first nettle

Make any difference as what grows

Becomes a skit? Three sides enclosed,

The fourth open to a wash of the weather,

Exits and entrances, gestures theatrically meant

To punctuate like doubled-over weeds as

The garden fills up with snow?

Ah, but this would have been another, quite other

Entertainment, not the metallic taste

In my mouth as I look away, density black as gunpowder

In the angles where the grass writing goes on,

Rose-red in unexpected places like the pressure

Of fingers on a book suddenly snapped shut.

Those tangled versions of the truth are

Combed out, the snarls ripped out

And spread around. Behind the mask

Is still a continental appreciation

Of what is fine, rarely appears and when it does is already

Dying on the breeze that brought it to the threshold

Of speech. The story worn out from telling.

All diaries are alike, clear and cold, with

The outlook for continued cold. They are placed

Horizontal, parallel to the earth,

Like the unencumbering dead. Just time to reread this

And the past slips through your fingers, wishing you

    were there.

Scheherazade

Unsupported by reason's enigma

Water collects in squared stone catch basins.

The land is dry. Under it moves

The water. Fish live in the wells. The leaves,

A concerned green, are scrawled on the light. Bad

Bindweed and rank ragweed somehow forget to flourish here.

An inexhaustible wardrobe has been placed at the disposal

Of each new occurrence. It can be itself now.

Day is almost reluctant to decline

And slowing down opens out new avenues

That don't infringe on space but are living here with us.

Other dreams came and left while the bank

Of colored verbs and adjectives was shrinking from the light

To nurse in shade their want of a method

But most of all she loved the particles

That transform objects of the same category

Into particular ones, each distinct

Within and apart from its own class.

In all this springing up was no hint

Of a tide, only a pleasant wavering of the air
In which all things seemed present, whether
Just past or soon to come. It was all invitation.
So much the flowers outlined along the night
Alleys when few were visible, yet
Their story sounded louder than the hum
Of bug and stick noises that brought up the rear,
Trundling it along into a new fact of day.
These were meant to be read as any
Salutation before getting down to business,
But they stuck to their guns, and so much
Was their obstinacy in keeping with the rest
(Like long flashes of white birds that refuse to die
When day does) that none knew the warp
Which presented this major movement as a firm
Digression, a plain that slowly becomes a mountain.

So each found himself caught in a net
As a fashion, and all efforts to wriggle free
Involved him further, inexorably, since all
Existed there to be told, shot through
From border to border. Here were stones
That read as patches of sunlight, there was the story

Of the grandparents, of the vigorous young champion

(The lines once given to another, now

Restored to the new speaker), dinners and assemblies,

The light in the old home, the secret way

The rooms fed into each other, but all

Was wariness of time watching itself

For nothing in the complex story grew outside:

The greatness in the moment of telling stayed unresolved

Until its wealth of incident, pain mixed with pleasure,

Faded in the precise moment of bursting

Into bloom, its growth a static lament.

Some stories survived the dynasty of the builders

But their echo was itself locked in, became

Anticipation that was only memory after all,

For the possibilities are limited. It is seen

At the end that the kind and good are rewarded,

That the unjust one is doomed to burn forever

Around his error, sadder and wiser anyway.

Between these extremes the others muddle through

Like us, uncertain but wearing artlessly

Their function of minor characters who must

Be kept in mind. It is we who make this

Jungle and call it space, naming each root,

Each serpent, for the sound of the name

As it clinks dully against our pleasure,

Indifference that is pleasure. And what would they be

Without an audience to restrict the innumerable

Passes and swipes, restored to good humor as it issues

Into the impervious evening air? So in some way

Although the arithmetic is incorrect

The balance is restored because it

Balances, knowing it prevails,

And the man who made the same mistake twice is exonerated.

Absolute Clearance

"Voilà, Messieurs, les spectacles que Dieu donne à l'univers..."

— Bossuet

He sees the pictures on the walls.

A sample of the truth only.

But one never has enough.

The truth doesn't satisfy.

In some vague hotel room

The linear blotches when dusk

Lifted them up were days and nights

And out over the ocean

The wish persisted to be a dream at home

Cloud or bird asleep in the trough

Of discursive waters.

The times when a slow horse along

A canal bank seems irrelevant and the truth:

The best in its best sample

Of time in relation to other time.

Suffer again the light to be displaced

To go down fuming

"So much is his courage high,

So vast his intelligence,

So glorious his destinies.

"Like an eagle that one sees always

Whether flying in the middle airs

Or alighting on some rock

Give piercing looks on all sides

To fall so surely on its prey

That one can avoid its nails

No less than its eyes."

How it would be clearer

Just to loaf, imagining little

(The fur of a cat in the sun):

Let the column of figures

Shift, add and subtract itself

(Sticks, numbers, letters)

And so on to median depth . . .

Until a room in some town

The result of a meeting therein

Clasping, unclasping

Toward the flustered look

Of toys one day put away for the last time.

"I put away childish things.

It was for this I came to Riverside

And lived here for three years

Now coming to a not uncertain

Ending or flowering as some would call it."

Teasing the blowing light

With its ultimate assurance

Severity of its curved smile

"Like the eagle

That hangs and hangs, then drops."

Grand Galop

All things seem mention of themselves
And the names which stem from them branch out to other referents.
Hugely, spring exists again. The weigela does its dusty thing
In fire-hammered air. And garbage cans are heaved against
The railing as the tulips yawn and crack open and fall apart.
And today is Monday. Today's lunch is: Spanish omelet, lettuce and
    tomato salad,
Jello, milk and cookies. Tomorrow's: sloppy joe on bun,
Scalloped corn, stewed tomatoes, rice pudding and milk.
The names we stole don't remove us:
We have moved on a little ahead of them
And now it is time to wait again.
Only waiting, the waiting: what fills up the time between?
It is another kind of wait, waiting for the wait to be ended.
Nothing takes up its fair share of time,
The wait is built into the things just coming into their own.
Nothing is partially incomplete, but the wait
Invests everything like a climate.
What time of day is it?

Does anything matter?

Yes, for you must wait to see what it is really like,

This event rounding the corner

Which will be unlike anything else and really

Cause no surprise: it's too ample.

Water

Drops from an air conditioner

On those who pass underneath. It's one of the sights of our town.

Puaagh. Vomit. Puaaaaagh. More vomit. One who comes

Walking dog on leash is distant to say how all this

Changes the minute to an hour, the hour

To the times of day, days to months, those easy-to-grasp entities,

And the months to seasons, which are far other, foreign

To our concept of time. Better the months—

They are almost persons—than these abstractions

That sift like marble dust across the unfinished works of the studio

Aging everything into a characterization of itself.

Better the cleanup committee concern itself with

Some item that is now little more than a feature

Of some obsolete style—cornice or spandrel

Out of the dimly remembered whole

Which probably lacks true distinction. But if one may pick it up,

Carry it over there, set it down,
Then the work is redeemed at the end
Under the smiling expanse of the sky
That plays no favorites but in the same way
Is honor only to those who have sought it.

The dog barks, the caravan passes on.
The words had a sort of bloom on them
But were weightless, carrying past what was being said.
"A nice time," you think, "to go out:
The early night is cool, but not
Too anything. People parading with their pets
Past lawns and vacant lots, as though these too were somehow
    imponderables
Before going home to the decency of one's private life
Shut up behind doors, which is nobody's business.
It does matter a little to the others
But only because it makes them realize how far their respect
Has brought them. No one would dare to intrude.
It is a night like many another
With the sky now a bit impatient for today to be over
Like a bored salesgirl shifting from foot to stockinged foot."
These khaki undershorts hung out on lines,

The wind billowing among them, are we never to make a
 statement?
And certain buildings we always pass which are never
 mentioned—
It's getting out of hand.
As long as one has some sense that each thing knows its place
All is well, but with the arrival and departure
Of each new one overlapping so intensely in the semi-darkness
It's a bit mad. Too bad, I mean, that getting to know each just for a
 fleeting second
Must be replaced by imperfect knowledge of the featureless whole,
Like some pocket history of the world, so general
As to constitute a sob or wail unrelated
To any attempt at definition. And the minor eras
Take on an importance out of all proportion to the story
For it can no longer unwind, but must be kept on hand
Indefinitely, like a first-aid kit no one ever uses
Or a word in the dictionary that no one will ever look up.
The custard is setting; meanwhile
I not only have my own history to worry about
But am forced to fret over insufficient details related to large
Unfinished concepts that can never bring themselves to the point
Of being, with or without my help, if any were forthcoming.

It is just the movement of the caravan away

Into an abstract night, with no

Precise goal in view, and indeed not caring,

That distributes this pause. Why be in a hurry

To speed away in the opposite direction, toward the other end of
    infinity?

For things can harden meaningfully in the moment of indecision.

I cannot decide in which direction to walk

But this doesn't matter to me, and I might as well

Decide to climb a mountain (it looks almost flat)

As decide to go home

Or to a bar or restaurant or to the home

Of some friend as charming and ineffectual as I am

Because these pauses are supposed to be life

And they sink steel needles deep into the pores, as though to say

There is no use trying to escape

And it is all here anyway. And their steep, slippery sides defy

Any notion of continuity. It is this

That takes us back into what really is, it seems, history—

The lackluster, disorganized kind without dates

That speaks out of the hollow trunk of a tree

To warn away the merely polite, or those whose destiny

Leaves them no time to quibble about the means,

Which are not ends, and yet . . . What precisely is it
About the time of day it is, the weather, that causes people to note it
    painstakingly in their diaries
For them to read who shall come after?
Surely it is because the ray of light
Or gloom striking you this moment is hope
In all its mature, matronly form, taking all things into account
And reapportioning them according to size
So that if one can't say that this is the natural way
It should have happened, at least one can have no cause for
    complaint
Which is the same as having reached the end, wise
In that expectation and enhanced by its fulfillment, or the
    absence of it.
But we say, it cannot come to any such end
As long as we are left around with no place to go.
And yet it has ended, and the thing we have fulfilled we have
    become.

Now it is the impulse of morning that makes
My watch tick. As one who pokes his head
Out from under a pile of blankets, the good and bad together,
So this tangle of impossible resolutions and irresolutions:

The desire to have fun, to make noise, and so to
Add to the already all-but-illegible scrub forest of graffiti on the
    shithouse wall.
Someone is coming to get you:
The mailman, or a butler enters with a letter on a tray
Whose message is to change everything, but in the meantime
One is to worry about one's smell or dandruff or lost glasses—
If only the curtain-raiser would end, but it is interminable.
But there is this consolation:
If it turns out to be not worth doing, I haven't done it;
If the sight appalls me, I have seen nothing;
If the victory is pyrrhic, I haven't won it.
And so from a day replete with rumors
Of things being done on the other side of the mountains
A nucleus remains, a still-perfect possibility
That can be kept indefinitely. And yet
The groans of labor pains are deafening; one must
Get up, get out and be on with it. Morning is for sissies like you
But the real trials, the ones that separate the men from the boys,
    come later.

Oregon was kinder to us. The streets
Offered a variety of directions to the foot

And bookstores where pornography is sold. But then
One whiffs just a slight odor of madness in the air.
They all got into their cars and drove away
As in the end of a movie. So that it finally made no difference
Whether this were the end or it was somewhere else:
If it had to be somewhere it might as well be
Here, on top of one. Here, as elsewhere,
April advances new suggestions, and one may as well
Move along with them, especially in view of
The midnight-blue light that in turning itself inside out
Offers something strange to the attention, a thing
That is not itself, gnat whirling before my eyes
At an incredible, tame velocity. Too pronounced after all
To be that meaningless. And so on to afternoon
On the desert, with oneself cleaned up, and the location
Almost brand-new what with the removal of gum wrappers, etc.
But I was trying to tell you about a strange thing
That happened to me, but this is no way to tell about it,
By making it truly happen. It drifts away in fragments.
And one is left sitting in the yard
To try to write poetry
Using what Wyatt and Surrey left around,
Took up and put down again

Like so much gorgeous raw material,

As though it would always happen in some way

And meanwhile since we are all advancing

It is sure to come about in spite of everything

On a Sunday, where you are left sitting

In the shade that, as always, is just a little too cool.

So there is whirling out at you from the not deep

Emptiness the word "cock" or some other, brother and sister words

With not much to be expected from them, though these

Are the ones that waited so long for you and finally left, having
    given up hope.

There is a note of desperation in one's voice, pleading for them,

And meanwhile the intensity thins and sharpens

Its point, that is the thing it was going to ask.

One has been waiting around all evening for it

Before sleep had stopped definitively the eyes and ears

Of all those who came as an audience.

Still, that poetry does sometimes occur

If only in creases in forgotten letters

Packed away in trunks in the attic—things you forgot you had

And what would it matter anyway,

That recompense so precisely dosed

As to seem the falling true of a perverse judgment.

You forget how there could be a gasp of a new air

Hidden in that jumble. And of course your forgetting

Is a sign of just how much it matters to you:

"It must have been important."

The lies fall like flaxen threads from the skies

All over America, and the fact that some of them are true of course

Doesn't so much not matter as serve to justify

The whole mad organizing force under the billows of correct
    delight.

Surrey, your lute is getting an attack of nervous paralysis

But there are, again, things to be sung of

And this is one of them, only I would not dream of intruding on

The frantic completeness, the all-purpose benevolence

Of that still-moist garden where the tooting originates:

Between intervals of clenched teeth, your venomous rondelay.

Ask a hog what is happening. Go on. Ask him.

The road just seems to vanish

And not that far in the distance, either. The horizon must have been
    moved up.

So it is that by limping carefully

From one day to the next, one approaches a worn, round stone
    tower

Crouching low in the hollow of a gully

With no door or window but a lot of old license plates

Tacked up over a slit too narrow for a wrist to pass through

And a sign: "Van Camp's Pork and Beans."

From then on in: *angst*-colored skies, emotional withdrawals

As the whole business starts to frighten even you,

Its originator and promoter. The horizon returns

As a smile of recognition this time, polite, unquestioning.

How long ago high school graduation seems

Yet it cannot have been so very long:

One has traveled such a short distance.

The styles haven't changed much,

And I still have a sweater and one or two other things I had then.

It seems only yesterday that we saw

The movie with the cows in it

And turned to one at your side, who burped

As morning saw a new garnet-and-pea-green order propose

Itself out of the endless bathos, like science-fiction lumps.

Impossible not to be moved by the tiny number

Those people wore, indicating they should be raised to this or that
 power.

But now we are at Cape Fear and the overland trail

Is impassable, and a dense curtain of mist hangs over the sea.

Poem in Three Parts

1. Love

"Once I let a guy blow me.

I kind of backed away from the experience.

Now years later, I think of it

Without emotion. There has been no desire to repeat,

No hangups either. Probably if the circumstances were right

It could happen again, but I don't know,

I just have other things to think about,

More important things. Who goes to bed with what

Is unimportant. Feelings are important.

Mostly I think of feelings, they fill up my life

Like the wind, like tumbling clouds

In a sky full of clouds, clouds upon clouds."

Nameless shrubs running across a field

That didn't drain last year and

Isn't draining this year to fall short

Like waves at the end of a lake,

Each with a little sigh,

Are you sure this is what the pure day

With its standing light intends?

There are so many different jobs:

It's sufficient to choose one, or a fraction of one.

Days will be blue elsewhere with their own purpose.

One must bear in mind one thing.

It isn't necessary to know what that thing is.

All things are palpable, none are known.

The day fries, with a fine conscience,

Shadows, ripples, underbrush, old cars.

The conscience is to you as what is known,

The unknowable gets to be known.

Familiar things seem a long way off.

2. Courage

In a diamond-paned checked shirt

To be setting out this way:

A blah morning

Not too far from home (home

Is a modest one-bedroom apartment,

City-owned and operated),

The average debris of the journey

Less than at first thought,

Smell of open water,

Troughs, special pits.

It all winds back again

In time for evening's torque:

So much we could have done,

So much we did do.

Weeds like skyscrapers against the blue vault of heaven:

Where is it to end? What is this? Who are these people?

Am I myself, or a talking tree?

3. I Love the Sea

There is no promise but lots

Of intimacy the way yellowed land narrows together.

This part isn't very popular

For some reason: the houses need repairs,

The cars in the yards are too new.

The enclosing slopes dream and are forgetful.

There are joyous, warm patches

Amid nondescript trees.

My dream gets obtuse:

When I woke up this morning I noticed first

That you weren't there, then prodded

Slowly back into the dream:

These trains, people, beaches, rides

In happiness because their variety

Is outlived but still there, outside somewhere,

In the side yard, maybe.

Ivy is blanketing one whole wall.

The time is darker

For fast reasons into everything, about what concerns it now.

We could sleep together again but that wouldn't

Bring back the profit of these dangerous dreams of the sea,

All that crashing, that blindness, that blood

One associates with other days near the sea

Although it persists, like the blindness of noon.

Voyage in the Blue

As on a festal day in early spring
The tidelands maneuver and the air is quick with imitations:
Ships, hats appear. And those,
The mind-readers, who are never far off. But
To get to know them we must avoid them.

And so, into our darkness life seeps,
Keeping its part of the bargain. But what of
Houses, standing ruined, desolate just now:
Is this not also beautiful and wonderful?
For where a mirage has once been, life must be.

The pageant, growing ever more curious, reaches
An ultimate turning point. Now everything is going to be
Not dark, but on the contrary, charged with so much light
It looks dark, because things are now packed so closely
    together.
We see it with our teeth. And once this

Distant corner is rounded, everything

Is not to be made new again. We shall be inhabited

In the old way, as ideal things came to us,

Yet in the having we shall be growing, rising above it

Into an admixture of deep blue enameled sky and bristly

    gold stars.

The way the date came in

Made no sense, it never had any.

It should have been a caution to you

To listen more carefully to the words

Under the wind as it moved toward us.

Perhaps, sinking into the pearl stain of that passionate eye

The minutes came to seem the excrement of all they were

    passing through,

A time when colors no longer mattered.

They are to us as qualities we were not meant to catch

As being too far removed from our closed-in state.

And ideally the chime of this

Will come to have the fascination of a remembered thing

Without avatars, or so remote, like a catastrophe

In some unheard-of country, that our concern

Will be only another fact in a long list of important facts.

You and I and the dog
Are here, this is what matters for now.
In other times things will happen that cannot possibly involve
    us now
And this is good, a true thing, perpendicular to the ground
Like the freshest, least complicated and earliest of memories.

We have them all, those people, and now they have us.
Their decision was limited, waiting for us to make the first
    move.
But now that we have done so the results are unfathomable, as
    though
A single implication could sway the whole universe on its stem.
We are fashionably troubled by this new edge of what had seemed
    finite

Before and now seems infinite though encircled by gradual
    doubts
Of whatever came over us. Perhaps the old chic was less barren,
More something to be looked forward to, than this
Morning in the orchards under an unclouded sky,

This painful freshness of each thing being exactly itself.

Perhaps all that is wanted is time.
People cover us, they are older
And have lived before. They want no part of us,
Only to be dying, and over with it.
Out of step with all that is passing along with them

But living with it deep into the midst of things.
It is civilization that counts, after all, they seem
To be saying, and we are as much a part of it as anybody else
Only we think less about it, even not at all, until some
Fool comes shouting into the forest at nightfall

News of some thing we know and care little of,
As the distant castle rejoices to the joyous
Sound of hooves, releasing rooks straight up into the faultless
    air
And meanwhile weighs its shadow ever heavier on the
    mirroring
Surface of the river, surrounding the little boat with three figures
    in it.

Farm

A protracted wait that is also night.
Funny how the white fence posts
Go on and on, a quiet reproach
That goes under as day ends
Though the geometry remains,
A thing like nudity at the end
Of a long stretch. "It makes such a difference."
OK. So is the "really not the same thing at all,"
Viewed through the wrong end of a telescope
And holding up that bar.

Living with the girl
Got kicked into the sod of things.
There was a to-do end of June,
Comings and goings
Before the matter is dropped.
But it stays around, like her faint point
Of frown, or the dripping leaves
Of pie-plant and hollyhock,
Also momentary in defeat.
No one has the last laugh.

Farm II

I was thinking

Now that the flowers are

                      forgotten

A whole new frontier

Backing around the old one are

Swamping its former good ideas

Plowing under the errors too

In its tin maelstrom: the overloaded

Ferryboat slowly moves away from the dock

Are these dog-eared things

Weeds what you call them

These things sitting like mail to be read

Toward the end of afternoon

Things the mailman brought

I would like to enroll

In the new course

At the study center

A lattice-work crust

Holes are blobs of darkness

Has been placed across the road

You can't walk out too far that way any more

They say the children are demolishing

The insides of the woods

                              burnt orange

That it's spectacular

But it doesn't

Take us out into the open sea

Only to the middle of a river

Fumbling which way to go.

Farm III

Small waves strike

The dark stones. The wife reads

The letter. There is nothing irreversible:

Points to the last sibilants

Of invading beef and calico.

Pretty soon oil has

Taken up the place of

The dark around you. It was all

As told, but anyway it never came out just right:

A fraction here, a lisp where it didn't matter.

It has to be presented

Through a final gap: pear trees and flowers

An ultimate resinous wall

Basking in the temperate climate

Of your identity. Sullen fecundity

To be watched over.

Hop o' My Thumb

The grand hotels, dancing girls

Urge forward under a veil of "lost illusion"

The deed to this day or some other day.

There is no day in the calendar

The dairy company sent out

That lets you possess it wildly like

The body of a dreaming woman in a dream:

All flop over at the top when seized,

The stem too slender, the top too loose and heavy,

Blushing with fine foliage of dreams.

The motor cars, tinsel hats,

Supper of cakes, the amorous children

Take the solitary downward path of dreams

And are not seen again.

What is it, Undine?

The notes now can scarcely be heard

In the hubbub of the flattening storm,

With the third wish unspoken.

I remember meeting you in a dark dream

Of April, you or some girl,

The necklace of wishes alive and breathing around your throat.

In the blindness of that dark whose

Brightness turned to sand salt-glazed in noon sun

We could not know each other or know which part

Belonged to the other, pelted in an electric storm of rain.

Only gradually the mounds that meant our bodies

That wore our selves concaved into view

But intermittently as through dark mist

Smeared against fog. No worse time to have come,

Yet all was desiring though already desired and past,

The moment a monument to itself

No one would ever see or know was there.

That time faded too and the night

Softened to smooth spirals or foliage at night.

There were sleeping cabins near by, blind lanterns,

Nocturnal friendliness of the plate of milk left for the fairies

Who otherwise might be less well disposed:

Friendship of white sheets patched with milk.

And always an open darkness in which one name

Cries over and over again: Ariane! Ariane!

Was it for this you led your sisters back from sleep

And now he of the blue beard has outmaneuvered you?

But for the best perhaps: let

Those sisters slink into the sapphire

Hair that is mounting day.

There are still other made-up countries

Where we can hide forever,

Wasted with eternal desire and sadness,

Sucking the sherbets, crooning the tunes, naming the names.

De Imagine Mundi

The many as noticed by the one:

The noticed one, confusing itself with the many

Yet perceives itself as an individual

Traveling between two fixed points.

Such glance as dares dart out

To pin you in your afternoon lair is only a reflex,

A speech in a play consisting entirely of stage directions

Because there happened to be a hole for it there.

Unfortunately, fewer than one half of one per cent

Recognized the divined gesture as currency

(Which it is, albeit inflated)

And the glance comes to rest on top of a steeple

With about as much interest as a bird's.

They had moved out here from Boston

Those two. (The one, a fair sample

Of the fair-sheaved many,

The other boggling into single oddness

Plays at it when he must

Not getting better or younger.)

The weather kept them at their small tasks:

Sorting out the news, mending this and that.

The great poker face impinged on them. And rejoiced

To be a living reproach to

Something new they've got.

Skeeter collecting info: "Did you know

About the Mugwump of the Final Hour?"

Their even flesh tone

A sign of "Day off,"

The buses moving along quite quickly on the nearby island

Also registered, as per his plan.

Taking a path you never saw before

Thought you knew the area

(The many perceive they fight off sleep).

"A few gaffers stay on

To the end of the line

Tho that is between bookends."

The note is struck finally

With just sufficient force but like a thunderbolt

As only the loudest can be imagined.

And they stay on to talk it over.

Foreboding

A breeze off the lake—petal-shaped
Luna-park effects avoid the teasing outline
Of where we would be if we were here.
Bombed out of our minds, I think
The way here is too close, too packed
With surges of feeling. It can't be.
The wipeout occurs first at the center,
Now around the edges. A big ugly one
With braces kicking the shit out of a smaller one
Who reaches for a platinum axe stamped excalibur:
Just jungles really. The daytime bars are
Packed but night has more meaning
In the pockets and side vents. I feel as though
Somebody had just brought me an equation.
I say, "I can't answer this—I know
That it's true, please believe me,
I can see the proof, lofty, invisible
In the sky far above the striped awnings. I just see
That I want it to go on, without
Anybody's getting hurt, and for the shuffling
To resume between me and my side of night."

The Tomb of Stuart Merrill

It is the first soir of March
They have taken the plants away.

Martha Hoople wanted a big "gnossienne" hydrangea
Smelling all over of Jicky for her
Card party: the basement couldn't
Hold up all that wildness.

The petits fours have left.

Then up and spake the Major:
The new conservatism is
Sitting down beside you.
Once when the bus slid out past Place Pereire
I caught the lens-cover reflection: lilacs
Won't make much difference it said.

Otherwise in Paris why
You never approved much of my pet remedies.

I spoke once of a palliative for piles

You wouldn't try or admit to trying any other.

Now we live without or rather we get along without

Each other. Each of us does

Live within that conundrum

We don't call living

Both shut up and open.

Can knowledge ever be harmful?

How about a mandate? I think

Of throwing myself on the mercy of the court.

They are bringing the plants back

One by one

In the interstices of heaven, earth and today.

"I have become attracted to your style. You seem to possess within your work an air of total freedom of expression and imagery, somewhat interesting and puzzling. After I read one of your poems, I'm always tempted to read and reread it. It seems that my inexperience holds me back from understanding your meanings.

"I really would like to know what it is you do to 'magnetize' your poetry, where the curious reader, always a bit puzzled, comes back for a clearer insight."

The canons are falling

One by one

Including "*le célèbre*" of Pachelbel

The final movement of Franck's sonata for piano and violin.

How about a new kind of hermetic conservatism

And suffering withdrawal symptoms of same?

Let's get on with it

But what about the past

Because it only builds up out of fragments.

Each evening we walk out to see

How they are coming along with the temple.

There is an interest in watching how

One piece is added to another.

At least it isn't horrible like

Being inside a hospital and really finding out

What it's like in there.

So one is tempted not to include this page

In the fragment of our lives

Just as its meaning is about to coagulate

In the air around us:

"Father!" "Son!" "Father I thought we'd lost you
In the blue and buff planes of the Aegean:
Now it seems you're really back."
"Only for a while, son, only for a while."
We can go inside now.

Tarpaulin

Easing the thing

Into spurts of activity

Before the emptiness of late afternoon

Is a kind of will power

Blaring back its received vision

From a thousand tenement windows

Just before night

Its signal fading

River

It thinks itself too good for
These generalizations and is
Moved on by them. The opposite side
Is plunged in shade, this one
In self-esteem. But the center
Keeps collapsing and re-forming.
The couple at a picnic table (but
It's too early in the season for picnics)
Are traipsed across by the river's
Unknowing knowledge of its workings
To avoid possible boredom and the stain
Of too much intuition the whole scene
Is walled behind glass. "Too early,"
She says, "in the season." A hawk drifts by.
"Send everybody back to the city."

Mixed Feelings

A pleasant smell of frying sausages
Attacks the sense, along with an old, mostly invisible
Photograph of what seems to be girls lounging around
An old fighter bomber, circa 1942 vintage.
How to explain to these girls, if indeed that's what they are,
These Ruths, Lindas, Pats and Sheilas
About the vast change that's taken place
In the fabric of our society, altering the texture
Of all things in it? And yet
They somehow look as if they knew, except
That it's so hard to see them, it's hard to figure out
Exactly what kind of expressions they're wearing.
What are your hobbies, girls? Aw nerts,
One of them might say, this guy's too much for me.
Let's go on and out, somewhere
Through the canyons of the garment center
To a small café and have a cup of coffee.
I am not offended that these creatures (that's the word)
Of my imagination seem to hold me in such light esteem,

Pay so little heed to me. It's part of a complicated

Flirtation routine, anyhow, no doubt. But this talk of

The garment center? Surely that's California sunlight

Belaboring them and the old crate on which they

Have draped themselves, fading its Donald Duck insignia

To the extreme point of legibility.

Maybe they were lying but more likely their

Tiny intelligences cannot retain much information.

Not even one fact, perhaps. That's why

They think they're in New York. I like the way

They look and act and feel. I wonder

How they got that way, but am not going to

Waste any more time thinking about them.

I have already forgotten them

Until some day in the not too distant future

When we meet possibly in the lounge of a modern airport,

They looking as astonishingly young and fresh as when this
    picture was made

But full of contradictory ideas, stupid ones as well as

Worthwhile ones, but all flooding the surface of our minds

As we babble about the sky and the weather and the forests of
    change.

The One Thing That Can Save America

Is anything central?

Orchards flung out on the land,

Urban forests, rustic plantations, knee-high hills?

Are place names central?

Elm Grove, Adcock Corner, Story Book Farm?

As they concur with a rush at eye level

Beating themselves into eyes which have had enough

Thank you, no more thank you.

And they come on like scenery mingled with darkness

The damp plains, overgrown suburbs,

Places of known civic pride, of civil obscurity.

These are connected to my version of America

But the juice is elsewhere.

This morning as I walked out of your room

After breakfast crosshatched with

Backward and forward glances, backward into light,

Forward into unfamiliar light,

Was it our doing, and was it

The material, the lumber of life, or of lives
We were measuring, counting?
A mood soon to be forgotten
In crossed girders of light, cool downtown shadow
In this morning that has seized us again?

I know that I braid too much my own
Snapped-off perceptions of things as they come to me.
They are private and always will be.
Where then are the private turns of event
Destined to boom later like golden chimes
Released over a city from a highest tower?
The quirky things that happen to me, and I tell you,
And you instantly know what I mean?
What remote orchard reached by winding roads
Hides them? Where are these roots?

It is the lumps and trials
That tell us whether we shall be known
And whether our fate can be exemplary, like a star.
All the rest is waiting
For a letter that never arrives,
Day after day, the exasperation

Until finally you have ripped it open not knowing what it is,

The two envelope halves lying on a plate.

The message was wise, and seemingly

Dictated a long time ago.

Its truth is timeless, but its time has still

Not arrived, telling of danger, and the mostly limited

Steps that can be taken against danger

Now and in the future, in cool yards,

In quiet small houses in the country,

Our country, in fenced areas, in cool shady streets.

Tenth Symphony

I have not told you

About the riffraff at the boat show.

But seeing the boats coast by

Just now on their truck:

All red and white and blue and red

Prompts me to, wanting to get in your way.

You've never told me about a lot of things:

Why you love me, why we love you, and just exactly

What sex is. When people speak of it

As happens increasingly, are they always

Referring to the kind where sexual organs are brought in—

Diffident, vague, hard to imagine as they are to a blind person?

I find that thinking these things divides us,

Brings us together. As on last Thanksgiving

Nobody could finish what was on his plate,

And gave thanks. Means more

To some than me I guess.

But again I'm not sure of that.

There is some connexion

(I like the way the English spell it

They're so clever about some things

Probably smarter generally than we are

Although there is supposed to be something

We have that they don't—don't ask me

What it is. And please no talk of openness.

I would pick Francis Thompson over Bret Harte

Any day, if I had to)

Among this. It connects up,

Not *to* anything, but kind of like

Closing the ranks so as to leave them open.

You can "stop and shop." Self service

And the honor system prevail, resulting in

Tremendous amounts of spare time,

A boon to some, to others more of a problem

That only points a way around it.

Sitting in the living room this afternoon I saw

How to use it. My vision remained etched in the

Buff wall a long time, an elective

Cheshire cat. Unable to cancel,

The message is received penultimately.

So over these past years—

A little puttering around,

Some relaxing, a lot of plans and ideas.

Hope to have more time to tell you about

The latter in the foreseeable future.

On Autumn Lake

Leading liot act to foriage is activity
Of Chinese philosopher here on Autumn Lake thoughtfully
    inserted in
Plovince of Quebec—stop it! I will not. The edge hugs
The lake with ever-more-paternalistic insistence, whose effect
Is in the blue way up ahead. The distance

By air from other places to here isn't much, but
It doesn't count, at least not the way the
Shore distance—leaf, tree, stone; optional (fern, frog, skunk);
And then stone, tree, leaf; then another optional—counts.
It's like the "machines" of the 19th-century Academy.
Turns out you didn't need all that training
To do art—that it was even better not to have it. Look at
The Impressionists—some of 'em had it, too, but preferred to
    forget it
In vast composed canvases by turns riotous
And indigent in color, from which only the notion of space

    is lacking.

I do not think that this

Will be my last trip to Autumn Lake

Have some friends among many severe heads

We all scholars sitting under tree

Waiting for nut to fall. Some of us studying

Persian and Aramaic, others the art of distilling

Weird fragrances out of nothing, from the ground up.

In each the potential is realized, the two wires

Are crossing.

Fear of Death

What is it now with me

And is it as I have become?

Is there no state free from the boundary lines

Of before and after? The window is open today

And the air pours in with piano notes

In its skirts, as though to say, "Look, John,

I've brought these and these"—that is,

A few Beethovens, some Brahmses,

A few choice Poulenc notes. . . . Yes,

It is being free again, the air, it has to keep coming back

Because that's all it's good for.

I want to stay with it out of fear

That keeps me from walking up certain steps,

Knocking at certain doors, fear of growing old

Alone, and of finding no one at the evening end

Of the path except another myself

Nodding a curt greeting: "Well, you've been awhile
But now we're back together, which is what counts."
Air in my path, you could shorten this,
But the breeze has dropped, and silence is the last word.

Ode to Bill

Some things we do take up a lot more time
And are considered a fruitful, natural thing to do.
I am coming out of one way to behave
Into a plowed cornfield. On my left, gulls,
On an inland vacation. They seem to mind the way
    I write.

Or, to take another example: last month
I vowed to write more. What is writing?
Well, in my case, it's getting down on paper
Not thoughts, exactly, but ideas, maybe:
Ideas about thoughts. Thoughts is too grand a word.
Ideas is better, though not precisely what I mean.
Someday I'll explain. Not today though.

I feel as though someone had made me a vest
Which I was wearing out of doors into the countryside
Out of loyalty to the person, although
There is no one to see, except me

With my inner vision of what I look like.

The wearing is both a duty and a pleasure

Because it absorbs me, absorbs me too much.

One horse stands out irregularly against

The land over there. And am I receiving

This vision? Is it mine, or do I already owe it

For other visions, unnoticed and unrecorded

On the great, relaxed curve of time,

All the forgotten springs, dropped pebbles,

Songs once heard that then passed out of light

Into everyday oblivion? He moves away slowly,

Looks up and pumps the sky, a lingering

Question. Him too we can sacrifice

To the end progress, for we must, we must be moving on.

Lithuanian Dance Band

Nathan the Wise is a good title it's a reintroduction
Of heavy seeds attached by toggle switch to long loops leading
Out of literature and life into worldly chaos in which
We struggle two souls out of work for it's a long way back to
The summation meanwhile we live in it "gradually getting
    used to"
Everything and this overrides living and is superimposed
    on it
As when a wounded jackal is tied to the waterhole the lion
    does come

I write you to air these few thoughts feelings you are
Most likely driving around the city in your little car
Breathing in the exquisite air of the city and the exhaust fumes
    dust and other
Which make it up only hold on awhile there will be time
For other decisions but now I want to concentrate on this
Image of you secure and projected how I imagine you
Because you are this way where are you you are in my thoughts

Something in me was damaged I don't know how or by what
Today is suddenly broad and a whole era of uncertainties is
ending
Like World War I or the twenties it keeps ending this is the
beginning
Of music afterward and refreshments all kinds of simple
delicacies
That toast the heart and create a rival ambiance of cordiality
To the formal one we are keeping up in our hearts the same

What with skyscrapers and dirigibles and balloons the sky
seems pretty crowded
And a nice place to live at least I think so do you
And the songs strike up there are chorales everywhere so pretty
it's lovely
And everywhere the truth rushes in to fill the gaps left by
Its sudden demise so that a fairly accurate record of its activity
is possible
If there were sex in friendship this would be the place to have it
right here on this floor
With bells ringing and the loud music pealing

Perhaps another day one will want to review all this

For today it looks compressed like lines packed together

In one of those pictures you reflect with a polished tube

To get the full effect and this is possible

I feel it in the lean reaches of the weather and the wind

That sweeps articulately down these drab streets

Bringing everything to a high gloss

Yet we are alone too and that's sad isn't it

Yet you are meant to be alone at least part of the time

You must be in order to work and yet it always seems so unnatural

As though seeing people were intrinsic to life which it just might be

And then somehow the loneliness is more real and more human

You know not just the scarecrow but the whole landscape

And the crows peacefully pecking where the harrow has passed

Sand Pail

Process

of a red stripe through much whiplash

of environmental sweepstakes misinterprets

slabs as they come forward. A

footprint

directs traffic in the center

of flat crocus plaza as the storm

incurves on this new situation. Why

are there developments?

A transparent shovel paves, "they" say,

residual elastic fetters

pictures of moments

brought under the sand.

No Way of Knowing

And then? Colors and names of colors,
The knowledge of you a certain color had?
The whole song bag, the eternal oom-pah refrain?
Street scenes? A blur of pavement
After the cyclists passed, calling to each other,
Calling each other strange, funny-sounding names?
Yes, probably, but in the meantime, waking up
In the middle of a dream with one's mouth full
Of unknown words takes in all of these:
It is both the surface and the accidents
Scarring that surface, yet it too only contains
As a book on Sweden only contains the pages of that book.
The dank no-places and the insubstantial pinnacles—
Both get carried away on the surface of a flood
That doesn't care about anything,
Not even about minding its own business.
There were holidays past we used to
Match up, and yep, they fitted together
All right, but the days in between grow rank,

Consume their substance, orphan, disinherit

But the air stands in curtains, reigns

Like a centennial. No one can get in or out.

These are parts of the same body:

One could possibly live without some

Such as a finger or elbow, but the head is

Necessary, and what is in doubt here. This

Morning it was off taking French lessons.

Now it is resting and cannot be disturbed.

Yes, but—there are no "yes, buts".

The body is what this is all about and it disperses

In sheeted fragments, all somewhere around

But difficult to read correctly since there is

No common vantage point, no point of view

Like the "I" in a novel. And in truth

No one never saw the point of any. This stubble-field

Of witnessings and silent lowering of the lids

On angry screen-door moment rushing back

To the edge of woods was always alive with its own

Rigid binary system of inducing truths

From starved knowledge of them. It has worked

And will go on working. All attempts to influence

The working are parallelism, undulating, writhing

Sometimes but kept to the domain of metaphor.

There is no way of knowing whether these are

Our neighbors or friendly savages trapped in the distance

By the red tape of a mirage. The fact that

We drawled "hallo" to them just lazily enough this morning

Doesn't mean that a style was inaugurated. Anyway evening

Kind of changes things. Not the color,

The quality of a handshake, the edge on someone's breath,

So much as a general anxiety to get everything all added up,

Flowers arranged and out of sight. The vehicular madness

Goes on, crashing, thrashing away, but

For many this is near enough to the end: one may

Draw up a chair close to the balcony railing.

The sunset is just starting to light up.

As when the songs start to go

Not much can be done about it. Waiting

In vanilla corridors for an austere

Young nurse to appear, an opaque glass vase of snapdragons

On one arm, the dangerously slender heroine

Backbending over the other, won't save the denouement

Already drenched in the perfume of fatality. The passengers

Reappear. The cut driver pushes them to heaven.

(Waterford explodes over the flagstones.)

At the same time that we are trying to spell out

This very simple word, put one note

After the other, push back the dead chaos

Insinuating itself in the background like mists

Of happy autumn fields—your money is dead.

I like the spirit of the songs, though,

The camaraderie that is the last thing to peel off,

Visible even now on the woven pattern of branches

And twilight. Why must you go? Why can't you

Spend the night, here in my bed, with my arms wrapped tightly
> around you?

Surely that would solve everything by supplying

A theory of knowledge on a scale with the gigantic

Bits and pieces of knowledge we have retained:

An LP record of all your favorite friendships,

Of letters from the front? Too

Fantastic to make sense? But it made the chimes ring.

If you listen you can hear them ringing still:

A mood, a Stimmung, adding up to a sense of what they really were,

All along, through the chain of lengthening days.

Suite

The inert lifeless mass calls out into space:
Seven long years and the wall hasn't been built yet
The crust thickens, the back of everything . . .
Clustered carillons and the pink dew of afterthoughts
Support it.

This was to be forgotten, eliminated
From history. But time is a garden wherein
Memories thrive monstrously until
They become the vagrant flowering of something else
Like stopping near the fence with your raincoat.

At night, orange mists.
The sun has killed a trillion of 'em
And it keeps stretching back, impossible planets.
How do I know? I'm lost. It says its name.
The blue-black message at the end of the garden
Is garbled. Meanwhile we're supposed to be here
Among pine trees and nice breaths of fresh air.

Snow was the last thing he'd expected.

Sun, and the kiss of far, unfamiliar lands,

Harsh accents though strangely kind

And now from the unbuttoned corner moving out,

Coming out, the postponed play of this day.

Astonishing. It really tells you about yourself,

The day made whole, the eye and the report together, silent.

Märchenbilder

Es war einmal . . . No, it's too heavy
To be said. Besides, you aren't paying attention any more.
How shall I put it?
"The rain thundered on the uneven red flagstones.

The steadfast tin soldier gazed beyond the drops
Remembering the hat-shaped paper boat, that soon . . ."
That's not it either.
Think about the long summer evenings of the past, the queen
    anne's lace.

Sometimes a musical phrase would perfectly sum up
The mood of a moment. One of those lovelorn sonatas
For wind instruments was riding past on a solemn white horse.
Everybody wondered who the new arrival was.

Pomp of flowers, decorations
Junked next day. Now look out of the window.
The sky is clear and bland. The wrong kind of day
For business or games, or betting on a sure thing.

The trees weep drops

Into the water at night. Slowly couples gather.

She looks into his eyes. "It would not be good

To be left alone." He: "I'll stay

As long as the night allows." This was one of those night
    rainbows

In negative color. As we advance, it retreats; we see

We are now far into a cave, must be. Yet there seem to be

Trees all around, and a wind lifts their leaves, slightly.

I want to go back, out of the bad stories,

But there's always the possibility that the next one . . .

No, it's another almond tree, or a ring-swallowing frog . . .

Yet they are beautiful as we people them

With ourselves. They are empty as cupboards.

To spend whole days drenched in them, waiting for the next
    whisper,

For the word in the next room. This is how the princes must have
    behaved,

Lying down in the frugality of sleep.

City Afternoon

A veil of haze protects this

Long-ago afternoon forgotten by everybody

In this photograph, most of them now

Sucked screaming through old age and death.

If one could seize America

Or at least a fine forgetfulness

That seeps into our outline

Defining our volumes with a stain

That is fleeting too

But commemorates

Because it does define, after all:

Gray garlands, that threesome

Waiting for the light to change,

Air lifting the hair of one

Upside down in the reflecting pool.

Robin Hood's Barn

This would be the day: a few small drops of rain,

A dab of this, a touch of eau-de-cologne air

As long as it's suggestive. And it

Mounts, a serenade, to the surrounding

Love. You bad birds,

But God shall not punish you, you

Shall be with us in heaven, though less

Conscious of your happiness, perhaps, than we.

Hell is a not quite satisfactory heaven, probably,

But you are the fruit and jewels

Of my arrangement: O be with me!

Forget stand-offishness, exact

Bookkeeping of harsh terms! The banal

Sun is about to creep across heaven on its

Daily turn: don't let it find us arguing

Or worse, alone, each

Having turned his back to the other,

Alone in the wonderful solitude

Of the new day. To be there

Is not to know it, its outline

Creeps up on you, and then it has fallen over you

Like bedclothes of fog.

From some serene, high table

Set near the top of a flight of stairs

Come once and for all into our

Consideration though it be flat like lemonade.

The rest that is dreamed is as the husk

Of this feast on the damp ground.

As I was turning to say something to her she sped by me

Which meant all is over in a few years: twenty-six,

    twenty-seven,

Who were those people

Who came down to the boat and met us that time?

And your young years become a kind of clay

Out of which the older, more rounded and also brusquer

Retort is fashioned, the greeting

That takes you into night

Like a lantern up ahead:

The "Where were you"s; meanwhile

The dark is waiting like so many other things,

Dumbness and voluptuousness among them.

It is good to be part of it

In the dream that is the kernel

Deep in it, the unpretentious, unblushing,

But also the steep side stretching far away:

For this we pay, for this

Tonight and every night.

But for the time being we are free

And meanwhile the songs

Protect us, in a way, and the special climate.

All and Some

And for those who understand:
We shifted that day, until there was no more
Coming out of the situation we had so imitated.
And now we had talked of it
Not as a human being, deeply polite and intelligent
Coming forward to speak things of dark concern
But as a merely interesting description of itself.

Thus all good intentions remain puny
Consigned as they are to the cold dews
And nagging climates of a life's blood.
Does grave dawn drape in a pattern of convolvulus
The next noon alters, dim or baldly untragic
Until the pattern comes to seem no more than footsteps,
Dry and gay, doting on the old-fashioned, the mensual.

"Climate" isn't a sign, but it could be
A by-product, an anonymous blue-collar suburb
In the great mildness that has taken over the air

With snapping cogs, deft reversals.
The blinded sun's got to answer for this
But meanwhile the housing's been built
And actually moved into, some of it.

But what I mean is there's no excuse
For always deducing the general from particulars,
Like spots on that sun. How many
Helpless wails have slid out orchestras
Across skittery dance floors until even
The dancers were there, waltzing lamely at first
But now static and buzzing like plaid? No one
Cares or uses the little station any more.
They are too young to remember
How it was when the late trains came in.
Violet sky grazing the gray hill-crests.
What laziness of appetite
Kept the buzzards circling, and when dawn came
Up it did so on four wheels, without excuses or fuss.

It is impossible to picture the firmness
Of relationships then. The slack
Was by definition taken up, and so

Everything was useful. People died

Delighted with the long wait,

Exhaled brief words into the afternoon, the hills:

Then sweetness was knocked down for the last time.

Do you remember how we used to gather

The woodruff, the woodruff? But all things

Cannot be emblazoned, but surely many

Can, and those few devoted

By a caprice beyond the majesty

Of time's maw live happy useful lives

Unaware that the universe is a vast incubator.

To sense this clearly is not to know it, alas—

Today the directions arrive from many separated realms

Conjoining at the place of a bare pedestal.

Too many armies, too many dreams, and that's

It. Goodbye, you say, until next time

And I build our climate until next time

But the sky frowns, and the work gets completed in a dream.

Oleum Misericordiae

To rub it out, make it less virulent

And a stab too at rearranging

The whole thing from the ground up.

Yes we were waiting just now

Yes we are no longer waiting.

Afterwards when I tell you

It's as though it all only happened

As siding of my story

I beg you to listen

You are already listening

It has shut itself out

And in doing so shut us accidentally in

And meanwhile my story goes well

The first chapter
     endeth

But the real story, the one

They tell us we shall probably never know

Drifts back in bits and pieces

All of them, it turns out

So lucky

Now we really know

It all happened by chance:

A chance encounter

The dwarf led you to the end of a street

And pointed flapping his arms in two directions

You forgot to misprize him

But after a series of interludes

In furnished rooms (describe wallpaper)

Transient hotels (mention sink and cockroaches)

And spending the night with a beautiful married woman

Whose husband was away in Centerville on business

(Mention this wallpaper: the purest roses

Though the creamiest and how

Her smile lightens the ordeal

Of the last 500 pages

Though you never knew her last name

Only her first: Dorothy)

You got hold of the water of life

Rescued your two wicked brothers Cash and Jethro

Who promptly stole the water of life

After which you got it back, got safely home,

Saved the old man's life

And inherited the kingdom.

But this was a moment

Under the most cheerful sun.

In poorer lands

No one touches the water of life.

It has no taste

And though it refreshes absolutely

It is a cup that must also pass

Until everybody

Gets some advantage, big or little

Some reason for having come

So far

Without dog or woman

So far alone, unasked.

Self-Portrait in a Convex Mirror

As Parmigianino did it, the right hand
Bigger than the head, thrust at the viewer
And swerving easily away, as though to protect
What it advertises. A few leaded panes, old beams,
Fur, pleated muslin, a coral ring run together
In a movement supporting the face, which swims
Toward and away like the hand
Except that it is in repose. It is what is
Sequestered. Vasari says, "Francesco one day set himself
To take his own portrait, looking at himself for that purpose
In a convex mirror, such as is used by barbers . . .
He accordingly caused a ball of wood to be made
By a turner, and having divided it in half and
Brought it to the size of the mirror, he set himself
With great art to copy all that he saw in the glass,"
Chiefly his reflection, of which the portrait
Is the reflection once removed.
The glass chose to reflect only what he saw
Which was enough for his purpose: his image

Glazed, embalmed, projected at a 180-degree angle.

The time of day or the density of the light

Adhering to the face keeps it

Lively and intact in a recurring wave

Of arrival. The soul establishes itself.

But how far can it swim out through the eyes

And still return safely to its nest? The surface

Of the mirror being convex, the distance increases

Significantly; that is, enough to make the point

That the soul is a captive, treated humanely, kept

In suspension, unable to advance much farther

Than your look as it intercepts the picture.

Pope Clement and his court were "stupefied"

By it, according to Vasari, and promised a commission

That never materialized. The soul has to stay where it is,

Even though restless, hearing raindrops at the pane,

The sighing of autumn leaves thrashed by the wind,

Longing to be free, outside, but it must stay

Posing in this place. It must move

As little as possible. This is what the portrait says.

But there is in that gaze a combination

Of tenderness, amusement and regret, so powerful

In its restraint that one cannot look for long.

The secret is too plain. The pity of it smarts,

Makes hot tears spurt: that the soul is not a soul,

Has no secret, is small, and it fits

Its hollow perfectly: its room, our moment of attention.

That is the tune but there are no words.

The words are only speculation

(From the Latin *speculum*, mirror):

They seek and cannot find the meaning of the music.

We see only postures of the dream,

Riders of the motion that swings the face

Into view under evening skies, with no

False disarray as proof of authenticity.

But it is life englobed.

One would like to stick one's hand

Out of the globe, but its dimension,

What carries it, will not allow it.

No doubt it is this, not the reflex

To hide something, which makes the hand loom large

As it retreats slightly. There is no way

To build it flat like a section of wall:

It must join the segment of a circle,

Roving back to the body of which it seems

So unlikely a part, to fence in and shore up the face

On which the effort of this condition reads

Like a pinpoint of a smile, a spark

Or star one is not sure of having seen

As darkness resumes. A perverse light whose

Imperative of subtlety dooms in advance its

Conceit to light up: unimportant but meant.

Francesco, your hand is big enough

To wreck the sphere, and too big,

One would think, to weave delicate meshes

That only argue its further detention.

(Big, but not coarse, merely on another scale,

Like a dozing whale on the sea bottom

In relation to the tiny, self-important ship

On the surface.) But your eyes proclaim

That everything is surface. The surface is what's there

And nothing can exist except what's there.

There are no recesses in the room, only alcoves,

And the window doesn't matter much, or that

Sliver of window or mirror on the right, even

As a gauge of the weather, which in French is

Le temps, the word for time, and which

Follows a course wherein changes are merely

Features of the whole. The whole is stable within

Instability, a globe like ours, resting

On a pedestal of vacuum, a ping-pong ball

Secure on its jet of water.

And just as there are no words for the surface, that is,

No words to say what it really is, that it is not

Superficial but a visible core, then there is

No way out of the problem of pathos vs. experience.

You will stay on, restive, serene in

Your gesture which is neither embrace nor warning

But which holds something of both in pure

Affirmation that doesn't affirm anything.

The balloon pops, the attention

Turns dully away. Clouds

In the puddle stir up into sawtoothed fragments.

I think of the friends

Who came to see me, of what yesterday

Was like. A peculiar slant

Of memory that intrudes on the dreaming model

In the silence of the studio as he considers

Lifting the pencil to the self-portrait.

How many people came and stayed a certain time,

Uttered light or dark speech that became part of you

Like light behind windblown fog and sand,

Filtered and influenced by it, until no part

Remains that is surely you. Those voices in the dusk

Have told you all and still the tale goes on

In the form of memories deposited in irregular

Clumps of crystals. Whose curved hand controls,

Francesco, the turning seasons and the thoughts

That peel off and fly away at breathless speeds

Like the last stubborn leaves ripped

From wet branches? I see in this only the chaos

Of your round mirror which organizes everything

Around the polestar of your eyes which are empty,

Know nothing, dream but reveal nothing.

I feel the carousel starting slowly

And going faster and faster: desk, papers, books,

Photographs of friends, the window and the trees

Merging in one neutral band that surrounds

Me on all sides, everywhere I look.

And I cannot explain the action of leveling,

Why it should all boil down to one

Uniform substance, a magma of interiors.

My guide in these matters is your self,

Firm, oblique, accepting everything with the same

Wraith of a smile, and as time speeds up so that it is soon

Much later, I can know only the straight way out,

The distance between us. Long ago

The strewn evidence meant something,

The small accidents and pleasures

Of the day as it moved gracelessly on,

A housewife doing chores. Impossible now

To restore those properties in the silver blur that is

The record of what you accomplished by sitting down

"With great art to copy all that you saw in the glass"

So as to perfect and rule out the extraneous

Forever. In the circle of your intentions certain spars

Remain that perpetuate the enchantment of self with self:

Eyebeams, muslin, coral. It doesn't matter

Because these are things as they are today

Before one's shadow ever grew

Out of the field into thoughts of tomorrow.

Tomorrow is easy, but today is uncharted,

Desolate, reluctant as any landscape

To yield what are laws of perspective

After all only to the painter's deep

Mistrust, a weak instrument though

Necessary. Of course some things

Are possible, it knows, but it doesn't know

Which ones. Some day we will try

To do as many things as are possible

And perhaps we shall succeed at a handful

Of them, but this will not have anything

To do with what is promised today, our

Landscape sweeping out from us to disappear

On the horizon. Today enough of a cover burnishes

To keep the supposition of promises together

In one piece of surface, letting one ramble

Back home from them so that these

Even stronger possibilities can remain

Whole without being tested. Actually

The skin of the bubble-chamber's as tough as

Reptile eggs; everything gets "programmed" there

In due course: more keeps getting included

Without adding to the sum, and just as one

Gets accustomed to a noise that

Kept one awake but now no longer does,

So the room contains this flow like an hourglass

Without varying in climate or quality

(Except perhaps to brighten bleakly and almost

Invisibly, in a focus sharpening toward death — more

Of this later). What should be the vacuum of a dream

Becomes continually replete as the source of dreams

Is being tapped so that this one dream

May wax, flourish like a cabbage rose,

Defying sumptuary laws, leaving us

To awake and try to begin living in what

Has now become a slum. Sydney Freedberg in his

Parmigianino says of it: "Realism in this portrait

No longer produces an objective truth, but a *bizarria*. . . .

However its distortion does not create

A feeling of disharmony. . . . The forms retain

A strong measure of ideal beauty," because

Fed by our dreams, so inconsequential until one day

We notice the hole they left. Now their importance

If not their meaning is plain. They were to nourish

A dream which includes them all, as they are

Finally reversed in the accumulating mirror.

They seemed strange because we couldn't actually see them.

And we realize this only at a point where they lapse

Like a wave breaking on a rock, giving up

Its shape in a gesture which expresses that shape.

The forms retain a strong measure of ideal beauty

As they forage in secret on our idea of distortion.
Why be unhappy with this arrangement, since
Dreams prolong us as they are absorbed?
Something like living occurs, a movement
Out of the dream into its codification.

As I start to forget it
It presents its stereotype again
But it is an unfamiliar stereotype, the face
Riding at anchor, issued from hazards, soon
To accost others, "rather angel than man" (Vasari).
Perhaps an angel looks like everything
We have forgotten, I mean forgotten
Things that don't seem familiar when
We meet them again, lost beyond telling,
Which were ours once. This would be the point
Of invading the privacy of this man who
"Dabbled in alchemy, but whose wish
Here was not to examine the subtleties of art
In a detached, scientific spirit: he wished through them
To impart the sense of novelty and amazement to the spectator"
(Freedberg). Later portraits such as the Uffizi
"Gentleman," the Borghese "Young Prelate" and

The Naples "Antea" issue from Mannerist

Tensions, but here, as Freedberg points out,

The surprise, the tension are in the concept

Rather than its realization.

The consonance of the High Renaissance

Is present, though distorted by the mirror.

What is novel is the extreme care in rendering

The velleities of the rounded reflecting surface

(It is the first mirror portrait),

So that you could be fooled for a moment

Before you realize the reflection

Isn't yours. You feel then like one of those

Hoffmann characters who have been deprived

Of a reflflection, except that the whole of me

Is seen to be supplanted by the strict

Otherness of the painter in his

Other room. We have surprised him

At work, but no, he has surprised us

As he works. The picture is almost finished,

The surprise almost over, as when one looks out,

Startled by a snowfall which even now is

Ending in specks and sparkles of snow.

It happened while you were inside, asleep,

And there is no reason why you should have

Been awake for it, except that the day

Is ending and it will be hard for you

To get to sleep tonight, at least until late.

The shadow of the city injects its own

Urgency: Rome where Francesco

Was at work during the Sack: his inventions

Amazed the soldiers who burst in on him;

They decided to spare his life, but he left soon after;

Vienna where the painting is today, where

I saw it with Pierre in the summer of 1959; New York

Where I am now, which is a logarithm

Of other cities. Our landscape

Is alive with filiations, shuttlings;

Business is carried on by look, gesture,

Hearsay. It is another life to the city,

The backing of the looking glass of the

Unidentified but precisely sketched studio. It wants

To siphon off the life of the studio, deflflate

Its mapped space to enactments, island it.

That operation has been temporarily stalled

But something new is on the way, a new preciosity

In the wind. Can you stand it,

Francesco? Are you strong enough for it?

This wind brings what it knows not, is

Self-propelled, blind, has no notion

Of itself. It is inertia that once

Acknowledged saps all activity, secret or public:

Whispers of the word that can't be understood

But can be felt, a chill, a blight

Moving outward along the capes and peninsulas

Of your nervures and so to the archipelagoes

And to the bathed, aired secrecy of the open sea.

This is its negative side. Its positive side is

Making you notice life and the stresses

That only seemed to go away, but now,

As this new mode questions, are seen to be

Hastening out of style. If they are to become classics

They must decide which side they are on.

Their reticence has undermined

The urban scenery, made its ambiguities

Look willful and tired, the games of an old man.

What we need now is this unlikely

Challenger pounding on the gates of an amazed

Castle. Your argument, Francesco,

Had begun to grow stale as no answer
Or answers were forthcoming. If it dissolves now
Into dust, that only means its time had come
Some time ago, but look now, and listen:
It may be that another life is stocked there
In recesses no one knew of; that it,
Not we, are the change; that we are in fact it
If we could get back to it, relive some of the way
It looked, turn our faces to the globe as it sets
And still be coming out all right:
Nerves normal, breath normal. Since it is a metaphor
Made to include us, we are a part of it and
Can live in it as in fact we have done,
Only leaving our minds bare for questioning
We now see will not take place at random
But in an orderly way that means to menace
Nobody—the normal way things are done,
Like the concentric growing up of days
Around a life: correctly, if you think about it.

A breeze like the turning of a page
Brings back your face: the moment
Takes such a big bite out of the haze

Of pleasant intuition it comes after.

The locking into place is "death itself,"

As Berg said of a phrase in Mahler's Ninth;

Or, to quote Imogen in *Cymbeline*, "There cannot

Be a pinch in death more sharp than this," for,

Though only exercise or tactic, it carries

The momentum of a conviction that had been building.

Mere forgetfulness cannot remove it

Nor wishing bring it back, as long as it remains

The white precipitate of its dream

In the climate of sighs flung across our world,

A cloth over a birdcage. But it is certain that

What is beautiful seems so only in relation to a specific

Life, experienced or not, channeled into some form

Steeped in the nostalgia of a collective past.

The light sinks today with an enthusiasm

I have known elsewhere, and known why

It seemed meaningful, that others felt this way

Years ago. I go on consulting

This mirror that is no longer mine

For as much brisk vacancy as is to be

My portion this time. And the vase is always full

Because there is only just so much room

And it accommodates everything. The sample

One sees is not to be taken as

Merely that, but as everything as it

May be imagined outside time—not as a gesture

But as all, in the refined, assimilable state.

But what is this universe the porch of

As it veers in and out, back and forth,

Refusing to surround us and still the only

Thing we can see? Love once

Tipped the scales but now is shadowed, invisible,

Though mysteriously present, around somewhere.

But we know it cannot be sandwiched

Between two adjacent moments, that its windings

Lead nowhere except to further tributaries

And that these empty themselves into a vague

Sense of something that can never be known

Even though it seems likely that each of us

Knows what it is and is capable of

Communicating it to the other. But the look

Some wear as a sign makes one want to

Push forward ignoring the apparent

Naïveté of the attempt, not caring

That no one is listening, since the light

Has been lit once and for all in their eyes

And is present, unimpaired, a permanent anomaly,

Awake and silent. On the surface of it

There seems no special reason why that light

Should be focused by love, or why

The city falling with its beautiful suburbs

Into space always less clear, less defined,

Should read as the support of its progress,

The easel upon which the drama unfolded

To its own satisfaction and to the end

Of our dreaming, as we had never imagined

It would end, in worn daylight with the painted

Promise showing through as a gage, a bond.

This nondescript, never-to-be defined daytime is

The secret of where it takes place

And we can no longer return to the various

Conflicting statements gathered, lapses of memory

Of the principal witnesses. All we know

Is that we are a little early, that

Today has that special, lapidary

Todayness that the sunlight reproduces

Faithfully in casting twig-shadows on blithe

Sidewalks. No previous day would have been like this.

I used to think they were all alike,

That the present always looked the same to everybody

But this confusion drains away as one

Is always cresting into one's present.

Yet the "poetic," straw-colored space

Of the long corridor that leads back to the painting,

Its darkening opposite—is this

Some figment of "art," not to be imagined

As real, let alone special? Hasn't it too its lair

In the present we are always escaping from

And falling back into, as the waterwheel of days

Pursues its uneventful, even serene course?

I think it is trying to say it is today

And we must get out of it even as the public

Is pushing through the museum now so as to

Be out by closing time. You can't live there.

The gray glaze of the past attacks all know-how:

Secrets of wash and finish that took a lifetime

To learn and are reduced to the status of

Black-and-white illustrations in a book where colorplates

Are rare. That is, all time

Reduces to no special time. No one

Alludes to the change; to do so might

Involve calling attention to oneself

Which would augment the dread of not getting out

Before having seen the whole collection

(Except for the sculptures in the basement:

They are where they belong).

Our time gets to be veiled, compromised

By the portrait's will to endure. It hints at

Our own, which we were hoping to keep hidden.

We don't need paintings or

Doggerel written by mature poets when

The explosion is so precise, so fine.

Is there any point even in acknowledging

The existence of all that? Does it

Exist? Certainly the leisure to

Indulge stately pastimes doesn't,

Any more. Today has no margins, the event arrives

Flush with its edges, is of the same substance,

Indistinguishable. "Play" is something else;

It exists, in a society specifically

Organized as a demonstration of itself.

There is no other way, and those assholes

Who would confuse everything with their mirror games

Which seem to multiply stakes and possibilities, or

At least confuse issues by means of an investing

Aura that would corrode the architecture

Of the whole in a haze of suppressed mockery,

Are beside the point. They are out of the game,

Which doesn't exist until they are out of it.

It seems like a very hostile universe

But as the principle of each individual thing is

Hostile to, exists at the expense of all the others

As philosophers have often pointed out, at least

This thing, the mute, undivided present,

Has the justification of logic, which

In this instance isn't a bad thing

Or wouldn't be, if the way of telling

Didn't somehow intrude, twisting the end result

Into a caricature of itself. This always

Happens, as in the game where

A whispered phrase passed around the room

Ends up as something completely different.

It is the principle that makes works of art so unlike

What the artist intended. Often he finds

He has omitted the thing he started out to say

In the first place. Seduced by flflowers,

Explicit pleasures, he blames himself (though

Secretly satisfied with the result), imagining

He had a say in the matter and exercised

An option of which he was hardly conscious,

Unaware that necessity circumvents such resolutions

So as to create something new

For itself, that there is no other way,

That the history of creation proceeds according to

Stringent laws, and that things

Do get done in this way, but never the things

We set out to accomplish and wanted so desperately

To see come into being. Parmigianino

Must have realized this as he worked at his

Life- obstructing task. One is forced to read

The perfectly plausible accomplishment of a purpose

Into the smooth, perhaps even bland (but so

Enigmatic) finish. Is there anything

To be serious about beyond this otherness

That gets included in the most ordinary

Forms of daily activity, changing everything

Slightly and profoundly, and tearing the matter

Of creation, any creation, not just artistic creation

Out of our hands, to install it on some monstrous, near

Peak, too close to ignore, too far

For one to intervene? This otherness, this

"Not-being-us" is all there is to look at

In the mirror, though no one can say

How it came to be this way. A ship

Flying unknown colors has entered the harbor.

You are allowing extraneous matters

To break up your day, cloud the focus

Of the crystal ball. Its scene drifts away

Like vapor scattered on the wind. The fertile

Thought-associations that until now came

So easily, appear no more, or rarely. Their

Colorings are less intense, washed out

By autumn rains and winds, spoiled, muddied,

Given back to you because they are worthless.

Yet we are such creatures of habit that their

Implications are still around *en permanence*, confusing

Issues. To be serious only about sex

Is perhaps one way, but the sands are hissing

As they approach the beginning of the big slide

Into what happened. This past

Is now here: the painter's

Reflected face, in which we linger, receiving

Dreams and inspirations on an unassigned

Frequency, but the hues have turned metallic,

The curves and edges are not so rich. Each person

Has one big theory to explain the universe

But it doesn't tell the whole story

And in the end it is what is outside him

That matters, to him and especially to us

Who have been given no help whatever

In decoding our own man-size quotient and must rely

On second-hand knowledge. Yet I know

That no one else's taste is going to be

Any help, and might as well be ignored.

Once it seemed so perfect—gloss on the fine

Freckled skin, lips moistened as though about to part

Releasing speech, and the familiar look

Of clothes and furniture that one forgets.

This could have been our paradise: exotic

Refuge within an exhausted world, but that wasn't

In the cards, because it couldn't have been

The point. Aping naturalness may be the first step

Toward achieving an inner calm

But it is the first step only, and often

Remains a frozen gesture of welcome etched

On the air materializing behind it,

A convention. And we have really
No time for these, except to use them
For kindling. The sooner they are burnt up
The better for the roles we have to play.
Therefore I beseech you, withdraw that hand,
Offer it no longer as shield or greeting,
The shield of a greeting, Francesco:
There is room for one bullet in the chamber:
Our looking through the wrong end
Of the telescope as you fall back at a speed
Faster than that of light to flatten ultimately
Among the features of the room, an invitation
Never mailed, the "it was all a dream"
Syndrome, though the "all" tells tersely
Enough how it wasn't. Its existence
Was real, though troubled, and the ache
Of this waking dream can never drown out
The diagram still sketched on the wind,
Chosen, meant for me and materialized
In the disguising radiance of my room.
We have seen the city; it is the gibbous
Mirrored eye of an insect. All things happen
On its balcony and are resumed within,

But the action is the cold, syrupy flow

Of a pageant. One feels too confined,

Sifting the April sunlight for clues,

In the mere stillness of the ease of its

Parameter. The hand holds no chalk

And each part of the whole falls off

And cannot know it knew, except

Here and there, in cold pockets

Of remembrance, whispers out of time.

图书在版编目（CIP）数据

凸面镜中的自画像：阿什贝利诗集 /（美）约翰·阿什贝利著；少况译. — 北京：北京联合出版公司，2022.10
 ISBN 978-7-5596-6423-5

Ⅰ.①凸… Ⅱ.①约… ②少… Ⅲ.①诗集—美国—现代 Ⅳ.① I712.25

中国版本图书馆 CIP 数据核字 (2022) 第 158318 号

凸面镜中的自画像：阿什贝利诗集

作　者：	［美］约翰·阿什贝利
译　者：	少况
策划机构：	雅众文化
策划人：	方雨辰
出品人：	赵红仕
特约编辑：	傅小龙
责任编辑：	徐樟
装帧设计：	PAY2PLAY

北京联合出版公司出版
（北京市西城区德外大街 83 号楼 9 层　100088）
北京联合天畅文化传播公司发行
山东临沂新华印刷物流集团有限责任公司印刷　新华书店经销
字数 44 千字　860 毫米 ×1092 毫米　1/32　7.5 印张
2022 年 10 月第 1 版　2022 年 10 月第 1 次印刷
ISBN 978-7-5596-6423-5
定价：58.00 元

版权所有，侵权必究
未经许可，不得以任何方式复制或抄袭本书部分或全部内容
本书若有质量问题，请与本公司图书销售中心联系调换。
电话：64258472-800

SELF-PORTRAIT IN A CONVEX MIRROR by John Ashbery
Copyright © John Ashbery, 1972, 1973, 1974, 1975
Published by arrangement with Georges Borchardt, Inc.
through Bardon-Chinese Media Agency
Simplified Chinese translation copyright © 2022
by Shanghai Elegance Books Co., Ltd.
ALL RIGHTS RESERVED.